SEVENS

WEEK 2:
EXPOSED

Scott Wallens

PUFFIN BOOKS

All quoted materials in this work were created by the author.
Any resemblance to existing works is accidental.

Exposed

Puffin Books
Published by the Penguin Group
Penguin Putnam Books for Young Readers,
345 Hudson Street, New York, New York 10014, U.S.A.
Penguin Books Ltd, 80 Strand, London WC2R 0RL, England
Penguin Books Australia Ltd, Ringwood, Victoria, Australia
Penguin Books Canada Ltd, 10 Alcorn Avenue, Toronto, Ontario, Canada M4V 3B2
Penguin Books (N.Z.) Ltd, 182-190 Wairau Road, Auckland 10, New Zealand

Penguin Books Ltd, Registered Offices: Harmondsworth, Middlesex, England

Published by Puffin Books,
a division of Penguin Putnam Books for Young Readers, 2002

3 5 7 9 10 8 6 4 2

Front cover photography copyright © 2001 David Roth/Stone
Back cover photography copyright (top to bottom) Stewart Cohen/Stone,
David Roth/Stone, David Rinella, Steve Belkowitz/FPG, Karan Kapoor/Stone,
David Lees/FPG, Mary-Arthur Johnson/FPG

Produced by 17th Street Productions,
an Alloy Online, Inc. company
151 West 26th Street
New York, NY 10001

17th Street Productions and associated logos
are trademarks and/or registered trademarks of Alloy Online, Inc.

ISBN 0-14-230099-3

Printed in the United States of America

THIS SERIES IS DEDICATED TO
THE MEMORY OF BLAKE WALLENS,
BELOVED HUSBAND AND FRIEND.

4/16/1970–9/11/2001

CHAPTER ONE

A ray of sunlight cuts through the air and bathes Jeremy Mandile in its new morning warmth. Jeremy smiles slowly. It's the smile of a person still hanging on to sleep—breathing in the spring-fresh scent of his flannel sheets. It's the smile of a person just kissed.

Jeremy rolls onto his back and stretches his arms out and above his head. Still smiling. Fragments of last night come back to him in his half-groggy state. The party. The noise. The cheesy dance song that was playing on the stereo. The catch of his heart as Josh leaned in to kiss him. The way he closed his eyes and his own eyelashes tickled his face just before their lips met.

It had felt like his first kiss.

Kiss. Josh.

Jeremy sits up straight in bed, his heart suddenly pounding. "I kissed a guy," he whispers, rubbing his hands over his face. He squeezes his eyes shut and, for an instant, prays it was just a dream.

1

"Jeremy!" his mom calls from downstairs. "Breakfast!"

God, it sounds like a line out of the *Growing Pains* reruns his sister is always watching on the Disney channel. Something the mother of two-point-five kids and the owner of a picket-fence-surrounded house would say. *And why not?* Jeremy thinks. Up until last night, that was what his mother was. The mother of two *straight* kids and the owner of a classic split-level surrounded by a . . . okay, a chain-link fence. But still.

Now everything is different. Jeremy kissed a guy. If his mother knew that, her pristine little world would crumble.

My pristine little world is going to crumble, Jeremy thinks, his whole body coiling with tension.

"What am I gonna do?" Jeremy asks himself, slipping out of bed and walking over to the full-length mirror on the back of his bedroom door. His golden retriever, Pablo, jumps up from his regular sleeping spot at the foot of the bed and immediately licks Jeremy's hand. Jeremy pats the dog absently on the head and lets him out of the room so he can go downstairs to breakfast. Once the door is closed again, Jeremy gazes at his face in the mirror. It looks the same—dark spiky hair, light brown eyes, irritating stubble he wakes up with every morning. He runs his hand over his chin, absently checking for zits that aren't there, and stares into his eyes. There is one thing different. Glaringly so. That certain brightness in his eyes that screams out, "I have a massive crush!"

I kissed Josh and I liked it, Jeremy thinks. *I liked it a lot.*

He takes a deep breath and stares at his reflection. How can this possibly be happening?

Jeremy has suspected for a long time that there is something . . . *different* about him. That he has, at the very least, a certain attraction to guys that his other guy friends do not have. That he isn't as turned on by girls as the other guys seem to be. But he's always been into things that guy's guys are into. He's on the football, basketball, and track teams. He doesn't mind the occasional testosterone-infested near brawl. He's even dating one of the beautiful girls. And he's always figured that one day it will all snap into place. That being close to a girl will feel right. Or at least feel more than dull.

But that's gone now. Because nothing else has ever felt so right as kissing Josh did last night.

"No," Jeremy tells himself as his heart starts to pound. "No, it's not right. It was just a momentary lapse of reason. Kissing Tara is right. She's the one I want."

But that kiss . . .

"Jeremy! Let's go!" his mother calls, a little more edge in her voice. "You're going to be late for pregame practice!"

As if snapped out of a dream, Jeremy suddenly feels awake for the first time. He glances at the picture on the nightstand—the one in the chintzy heart-shaped frame that has *love* spelled out across the top in silver letters. It was given to him by Tara, his girlfriend, last Valentine's Day. In it is a picture of the two of them. Jeremy and Tara.

Tara—the sweet, funny, perfect, beautiful girl who is his best friend in the world. The girl who trusts him with everything—with her secrets, her fears, her heart. A fairly sizable lump forms in Jeremy's throat. He cheated on her. He's never thought of himself as a person who would cheat. But that's what he's done. And with a *guy*. What will she do if she finds out? Will she ever be able to even look at him again?

Jeremy crosses the room and picks up the frame, uses the corner of his sheet to wipe off a few fingerprints. His heart thumps at the sight of Tara's smiling face, the dimples his fingertips have traced so many times. He loves her. He's sure of that. How can all of this be happening?

He replaces the frame and returns his attention to his reflection, staring as deeply into his own eyes as possible.

"It's time to get a grip, my friend," Jeremy says. "You do not want *Josh*. You do not want a *guy*. You love Tara." He squares his shoulders and narrows his eyes. All he has to do is forget that last night ever happened. This is his life. Football. Tara. Normalcy.

• • •

By the time Meena turns onto Mission Avenue on Saturday morning, her eyes are refusing to stay open. She has to concentrate to keep them from closing. Oddly, the rest of her body doesn't feel all that tired.

Actually, it's not that odd, Meena thinks. *Considering you've had about thirty cups of coffee in the last twelve hours.*

Her heart is pounding a jittery caffeinated beat and it's quite possible that if her eyes did close, the rest of her would just keep blindly moving forward. She's too tired to even think about what she's going home to. Too physically exhausted to register dread. Meena crunches through a pile of dry brown leaves and she suddenly feels a vague sense of nostalgia, accompanied by a fuzzy twinge—as if she's forgotten something important. Something big. She looks at her chunky black watch, and the numbers blur before her weary eyes. She forces herself to focus. It's 8:45 A.M. Saturday. Right. Saturday morning. Swim meet. Ever since she can remember, she's always had a swim meet on Saturday morning.

Always. At least until she quit the team last week. When everything started to fall apart.

Meena stops, recognizing the mailbox in front of her. Shiny white, with little blue flowers and a big, gold 34. She's home. After an entire night of sitting at the Falls Diner on the sticky vinyl bench with a spring stabbing into her back and that freaky-looking tattoo guy staring at her through his one non-glass eye, she's finally home.

She wishes like hell she was back at the diner.

Before she gets halfway up the front walk, her mother is there in a cloud of lilac-scented soap and frizzy brown hair. She's grasping Meena with her bony arms. The woman has a grip that would make any WWF wrestler proud, even though she has the build of a ballet dancer.

"Where have you been?" her mother cries, all panic as she pulls back. She pushes Meena's hair away from her forehead and bends at the knees so she can look into her eyes—no, *search* her eyes—her other hand still gripping Meena's shoulder.

She's checking to see if I'm on drugs, Meena realizes, her heart giving a disappointed thud. *My mother thinks I'm on drugs.*

"Your eyes are all red," her mother says finally, standing up straight and crossing her arms over her tiny chest. "Meena, where have you been?"

"It's not what you think, Mom," Meena says, pushing past her mother. With any luck, she can get to her room without seeing her father. Or worse, Steven and Lydia.

"Don't take that tone with me, Meena," her mother says, like she's talking to a small child. "Not after keeping us all awake all night worried sick."

Her mother follows her into the house, where, of course, her father and Lydia and Steven Clayton are standing around the front door in a little arc, concerned expressions on each of their faces. Meena freezes, then instinctively takes a step closer to her father, away from Steven.

Stop looking at me, she mentally shouts in Steven's direction as she lets a blanket of hair fall in front of her face. *I don't want your eyes on me.*

"Meena? Are you even listening to me?" her mother shouts. Meena stares at the tiles on the floor—starts counting

6

the little marble squares. *One, two, three, four . . . Dad's foot . . . five, six—*

"I've been making phone calls since midnight, waking up all of your friends looking for you. Your father and Steven were out in their cars till all hours, scouring every inch of town—"

Meena can't take this anymore. She can feel him watching her. Even though she can't see him, she knows exactly what his eyes are saying. Poor Meena. Lovely Meena. Poor Meena needs taking care of.

"Leave me alone!" Meena shouts, surprising her mother into silence and shocking even herself. She hurls herself between her dad and Lydia, down the hall, and is on the stairs in a breath. *Just get to your room. Get in there, lock the door, and you'll be fine.*

"I'll go talk to her," she hears Steven say as her foot hits the third step.

Meena stops; her toe hits the rim of the next step and slips off, dropping her knee down to the edge of the step above it. Pain shoots through her kneecap and down her shin and Meena grips the banister to keep from crying out. There's no way she's going up to her room alone with Steven Clayton. She runs up the stairs.

She hears his footsteps coming down the hall, heading for the stairs, and briefly considers climbing out her bedroom window. She'd have nowhere to go but down once she gets out there, but a broken ankle wouldn't be so bad.

Meena wonders what the sensation of a broken bone feels like and suddenly recalls the image of her older brother's pinkie bone sticking out of the side of his hand when he was injured during a volleyball game three years ago. Then the phone rings.

"Who's calling us now?" her mother says. Meena freezes outside her bedroom, listening. She hears the sound of the phone being removed from its cradle. The sound of the beep as the talk button is pressed. But no more footsteps. Steven has stopped. Meena's heart quits trying to slam its way through her rib cage.

"Hello? Oh, hello, Chief Flaherty."

And her heart starts up again. Meena walks over to the staircase, descends the stairs, and walks through the dining room, away from Steven, to the door that leads to the kitchen. She stands in the open doorway. Her mother's back is to her as she talks on the cordless phone. Her father stands in the other doorway—the one bordering the foyer—and watches her. She can't help thinking there's a bit of fear in his eyes. Like she's something to be feared. Meena can barely swallow.

"Wait, I don't understand," her mother says, looking over at her dad. "You're telling me faulty wires started the fire?"

Meena's palms start to sweat. This can't be happening. Now they're going to know she lied. They're all going to know that she didn't start the fire that burned the

Claytons' house to a shell. How did the fire department figure it out so fast? And why did they have to be so damn thorough?

Meena wants Steven to think she started the fire to punish him. To get back at him for what he's done to her. She wants her parents to wake up and realize that something really bad happened to their daughter. She's not going through a phase. She's not rebelling. There's something wrong. And it has nothing to do with them or their parenting skills, or with the fact that she's adopted and they're white and she's Vietnamese. She wants things to go back to being right.

Meena's mother hangs up the phone and Meena can see that her hand is shaking. "Where is she?" her mother asks her dad. He simply lifts his chin in Meena's direction to tell her that Meena is behind her.

When her mother turns around, her expression is almost more than Meena can bear. It's the expression of a person who's just found out that her beloved child is actually a psychotic freak of nature.

"Why did you—" Meena's mother pauses to take in some air. "Why did you tell us you started the fire? Who would lie about such a thing?"

• • •

"Could this day be any more perfect?" Karyn Aufiero asks, reaching her arms above her head and stretching her fingers toward the clear blue sky until her back cracks.

There's not much in this world that Karyn loves more than a crisp-but-not-too-cold fall day and a football game. She reaches behind her head, bending her back until her fingertips press into the ribbed aluminum of the bleachers and her dirty-blond ponytail gently brushes the step. Then she kicks up her legs, first her right, then her left, executing a slow, perfect back walkover that stretches and compresses every muscle in her upper body. Karyn feels strong. And she relishes that feeling.

"Come on, Pretzel Girl," Karyn's best friend Amy Santisi says, tossing a half-used roll of yellow streamers back into the bag all the cheerleading decorations are kept in. "We're done with this side. Let's go help Jeannie and Gemma so we can get out of here. I need my maple syrup fix."

Karyn sighs and looks down the bleachers to the far corner, where Jeannie Chang and Gemma Masters are blowing up blue and yellow balloons and taping them to the railings. She's been avoiding Gemma all morning, wanting to sustain her good mood. She knows that if Gemma gets all three of them together, she's going to tell them every gory detail of what happened last night when she and her boyfriend, Carlos, had her house all to themselves. Karyn wouldn't mind hearing about Gemma and Carlos's sex life all the time if she didn't know what always came right afterward—instant obliteration of her good mood.

Unable to come up with a plausible reason for spending the next few hours at the top of the bleachers by herself,

Karyn follows Amy down the steps, her feet making loud, metallic reverberations as they smack down on the aluminum.

"Need help?" Amy asks, dropping onto the bottom bleacher and splaying her legs out in a manner that would get all of the six-hundred-plus guys at Falls High salivating for a look under her cheerleading skirt.

"Nah, we're almost done," Gemma says, pushing both hands through her short, red hair.

Good, Karyn thinks. *Maybe Amy and I can get out of here before the play-by-play happens.* She and Amy always go to the diner after decorating on Saturday mornings and order pancakes and bacon with tons of OJ—fueling up for the game. Gemma and Jeannie usually avoid joining in so they won't be tempted by the heavy food. It's the perfect excuse to escape the impending conversation. Karyn's about to open her mouth to suggest they go when Jeannie snatches away her golden opportunity.

"So Gemma, are you going to tell us about last night or what?" Jeannie says, perching on the bleacher next to Amy. Her long black hair whips around her face as a breeze kicks up, and a big chunk of it gets caught in her lip gloss. Jeannie scrunches up her nose and slowly pulls the hair away, twisting it back behind her head. "We're all dying of suspense."

Amy shoots Karyn a sarcastic look. *Here we go,* Karyn thinks.

"Oh, you guys don't want to hear about it," Gemma says, blushing and grinning from ear to ear as she ties the little balloon bag shut.

"Nope, but you want to tell us, so spill," Amy says, leaning her elbows back on the bleacher seat behind her. "I'm hungry already."

Karyn snorts a laugh as Gemma hurls the bag at Amy's head. She seems to think Amy is kidding—which she is—but only partly. Amy doesn't move and the balloons fall with a plop beneath the bleachers.

"I'm not getting that," Jeannie announces.

"Don't worry about it," Gemma says, standing in front of the three of them like she's about to give a lecture. "So . . . let's just say last night was not my finest hour," she says, placing her hands on her hips.

If it wasn't your finest hour, then why the grin? Karyn thinks. But she knows why. It's because Gemma thinks any sexual act is worth showing off about.

"Carlos did something . . . ugh! I don't even want to tell you guys about it," Gemma says, squeezing her eyes shut and shielding them with her hand.

"Come *on!*" Jeannie says, right on cue. "You can't back out now."

"Okay, so he comes over and I have this amazing dinner all laid out," Gemma says. "I made chicken Alfredo, Italian bread, salad . . . I even grabbed one of my parents' bottles of wine. That was my first mistake."

"Please don't tell me he tried to belch the state names in alphabetical order again," Amy interrupts, bending to retie her sneaker.

"Worse," Gemma says, holding out a flat hand to enunciate her point. "We go upstairs and I'm all psyched. You know, it's going to be the first time ever when we don't have to worry about anyone walking in, or about making too much noise. Everything was going to be perfect."

Gemma stops for dramatic tension.

"And?" Karyn prompts. It's not that she wants to ruin Gemma's moment, but . . . well, yes, she does, actually.

"And he lasted about two-point-five seconds," Gemma says.

Amy throws her arms in the air. "A new record!" she exclaims.

"It was the wine," Jeannie says, nodding and gazing at Gemma with the sympathetic expression of an older, wizened woman who could have imparted this information if only Gemma had thought to consult her first.

"It was the wine," Gemma agrees. "But that's not the worst of it. After he was done, he rolled over and said, 'Babe, could you get me some water? I think the chicken was salty.'" Gemma imitates Carlos's deep, lilting voice perfectly.

"Come *on!*" Karyn says. Even she can't stay quiet for that one.

"Loser," Jeannie adds under her breath.

"Guys can be such dicks," Karyn says.

"Please!" Gemma says. "Like you would know. T. J. Frasier is practically a model boyfriend."

Jeannie turns sideways on the bench and lies back, looking up at the sky. "Well, that's probably because they don't start being *real* dicks until after you have sex with them," she says.

And there it is, Karyn thinks, tempted to look at her watch to find out how long it took them, exactly, to get around to her virgin status.

"I still can't believe you haven't done it with T. J. Frasier," Gemma comments, bending to the ground to stretch out her thighs. She always says T. J.'s whole name like he's some kind of rock star whose name demands reverence. "What are you waiting for? His body is never going to be any more perfect than it is right now."

Karyn pushes herself away from the bleachers and starts to stretch out, too, even though she already spent thirty minutes this morning getting limber in her living room. She knows this conversation well enough to recite it in her head and she's sick of it already. These are her best friends. Can't they tell that she's sick of it already?

Karyn brings her face down to touch her right knee and closes her eyes. Instantly her mind flashes on an image of Reed Frasier and she smiles. She knows why her brain conjured him up at this precise moment—because Reed is a true best friend. He's her confidant. A person who really listens to her. A person who would never press her for the details of her PG-rated sex life. And not just because her boyfriend is his older brother.

A lot of people think it's odd that Karyn is so close with her boyfriend's little brother. But Karyn's been friends with Reed forever. Or at least since kindergarten, when he defended her against Doug Anderson, who was the biggest bully on the playground at the time. Reed is the reason Karyn noticed T. J. She'd spent so much time at the Frasier house last year, she and T. J. had ended up hanging out every other day. And then finally, one day when Reed had left them alone to take a rather long phone call, T. J. had kissed her.

And from that point on she and T. J. were together. But that's not going to stop her from being close to her best friend.

"Guys, I've told you. I'm just waiting for the right time," Karyn says, keeping her head down and moving to her left knee so she won't have to lie directly to their faces. Truth is, there have been plenty of right times. But unlike Gemma and Jeannie, she doesn't think about sex 24/7. She loves T. J., but when she even approaches the thought of having sex with him, she just freezes up and has to think about something else. She doesn't know why—that's just the way her brain works on that particular topic. But the one time she tried to explain that to her friends, they just didn't get it. And there's no way she wants to have *that* frustrating conversation again.

"Aren't you worried he's going to do it with some college girl?" Jeannie asks. She says it with no malice, no drama. Just asking a question as if it were the most obvious question in the world.

Karyn's heart squeezes down to the size of a Ping-Pong ball. She hadn't thought of that. How could she have never thought of that? T. J. is a hotshot freshman football prospect at Boston College. There are probably a million girls salivating over him at this very moment. What if Karyn keeps holding out and T. J. starts having sex with some older girl? No . . . some older *woman*. Girls are considered women in college, aren't they? Karyn's brain instantly flashes on a sophisticated, studious-looking redheaded hottie with the body of Denise Richards, lowering herself onto T. J.'s lap in front of a study carrel. What if T. J. decides Karyn's not worth waiting for and dumps her? What if—

"Guys, let's talk about something else, okay?" Amy says. She sits up straight and shoots Karyn a sympathetic look. "Like what are we going to do about that stupid hello cheer? I mean if we—"

"Omigod! That *stupid* hello cheer!" Jeannie exclaims. "We can't do it. It's *embarrassing!*"

Karyn resists the urge to kiss Amy in thanks, her mind already flitting away from the Denise Richards look-alike and onto the issue of the squad's opening pyramid. She reaches up and swipes the sleeve of her cheerleading sweater across her moist forehead. At least the hello cheer topic won't make her sweat uncontrollably.

• • •

Sunday evening Danny Chaiken finds himself staring at a knot in the wood surface of his musty, rickety old desk. He's been staring at it for some time, and as he narrows his eyes, he realizes that he can't remember what he was thinking about moments before. He picks his chin up off his folded arms and leans back in his chair, rubbing his palms against the legs of his baggy jeans repeatedly as if he's trying to get his blood flowing.

I know I was thinking about something. Danny racks his brain, scrunching his brows together in an effort to focus. School? Music? His parents? His sisters? Cori? What the hell was it? But it's no use. His brain is a fog of nothing.

But now that he's thought about it, maybe he should think about Cori. Just for a little while. He lets his thoughts wander off into his favorite fantasy about Cori Lerner. The one where she shows up at his house on a rainy night, her dark hair plastered to her face, her black T-shirt clinging to her body. He opens the door and she stands there, distraught, confessing that she couldn't wait a moment longer to tell him that she loves him. That she's always loved him. And then he grabs her, pulls her to him, and kisses her so passionately that she actually moans.

Just as Danny's getting into the daydream, it fades

away. He tries to draw it back, but the fog has taken over again. He can't make himself picture Cori or feel her. She's gone. Just like that.

Danny looks down at the pencil in his hand and for a split second wonders why it's there. Then he looks at his desk and sees the music composition paper he was leaning on. The few notes he had scribbled down are smudged, and Danny looks them over, hums a few bars, then crumples the paper into his fist as tightly as he possibly can. He opens his hand and looks at the little red half-moons he's made in the fleshy part of his hand. He stares. He doesn't feel a thing.

"Dammit!" Danny shouts, hurtling the paper across the room, where it bounces against a dozen other balls just like it and comes to rest at the feet of the huge SpongeBob SquarePants doll his little sisters gave him for his last birthday. He shouts just for the sake of shouting. He doesn't feel the urge to shout, nor the anger a shout would seem to imply. He doesn't feel anything. Danny lets his head fall to the desk, slapping his forehead against its hard surface.

"Ow," he says into the wood. "Felt that."

There's a knock at his door and it opens. Danny doesn't need to look up to know it's his mother. She's the only one who has that annoying habit. His father would never do it, out of respect for his privacy, and his sisters wouldn't do it, out of fear. Not of him, but of his black walls, his wide array of Slipknot and Outkast posters, the reptiles he keeps in fish tanks by the window, and the life-size Wolverine and Darth Maul cardboard cutouts that guard his bed. Jenny and Abby haven't really ventured into his room since he outgrew his Rugrats bedsheets.

"Why bother knocking if you're just going to walk in, anyway?" Danny says into the desk. Again, no feeling behind it, but he tries to make it sound biting.

"Nice tone," his mother says.

Guess it worked, Danny thinks.

He turns his face, still keeping contact between head and desk, and looks up out of the corner of his eye. As always, dear old Mom looks like she just stepped out of the pages of the *Good Housekeeping* magazines she keeps in the little flowered basket in the bathroom. Dyed blond hair tucked behind her ears, burgundy T-shirt topped by a burgundy-and-blue-plaid button-down, left open and casual since it's Sunday. The only thing separating her from the dronelike Martha Stewart wanna-bes in her rags is the perpetually irritated expression on her face whenever she's around her number-one son.

"What do you want?" Danny asks, knowing it will get under her skin.

"I was just wondering what you've been doing up here in your room alone all day," his mother says, glancing around systematically at each corner of his messy bedroom. Her eyes rest on his pile of cast-off paper balls. "But I see you've just been . . . what . . . wasting trees?"

"Ha ha," Danny says. He finally picks up his head, though it takes some effort, and pushes back from his desk. "I've been *trying* to do my homework, but I can't." He looks up at his mother, hoping this conversation won't be as futile as all the other ones he's had with her. Maybe just this once—

"*Can't,*" she says back sarcastically, and he knows all hope is already lost. "And I suppose your medication has something to do with it?"

"Whatever, don't believe me," Danny says, crossing his arms over his chest and tucking his hands under his arms. He pinches at the fleshy skin on his sides. He's been doing this a lot lately—constantly pinching his skin, tapping his thighs, pounding his head now and then—just hoping for some sensation. It doesn't exactly jump-start any emotions, but at least it's something. There was a time, not that long ago, when a conversation like this one would already have him so pissed off, he'd be storming around the room. But now he can't even get up enough ire to get out of his chair.

"All I know is I can't even think straight," Danny says, hazarding a glance at his mother's weary face. "How am I supposed to be creative when I . . ." How can he explain this to someone who can't possibly understand? Danny searches for the words to describe the heavy sort of numbness he's experiencing. "It's like I'm moving in a cloud," he says finally, hating the clichéd sound of it. "It's like all my senses are numbed."

His mom is fed up. "Danny—"

"Mom, I'm telling you, I can't feel angry, I can't feel happy, I can't feel sad." With each sentence he gives himself another pinch as an incentive to keep going. "I don't know what the hell I am if I can't feel anything. Am I even a person if I have no emotions? I mean, is that *good*? Is that what you really want for me?" He knows he's rambling, but he has to get through to her. He can't stay on this medication. He can't keep moving through life like a worthless blob. But his mother is shaking her head, scrunching her eyes. He's losing her, if he ever had her. "Mom—"

"Danny, I can't listen to this anymore," she says, throwing up her hands as if she's going to cover her ears. But she doesn't get quite that dramatic.

Then Danny does feel something. It's light and it's vague, but it's got shades of disappointment and self-pity.

"Fine, get out, then," he says, going for anger. He knows he should feel it; might as well pretend. His mother just stands there, looking at him like she wants to take something back. Obviously nothing she just said. It's all been said so many times, there couldn't possibly be a way to take it back. *Maybe she wants to take* everything *back,* Danny thinks. *My whole life. Me. Maybe she wants to go back and not have me.* Part of him wouldn't blame her.

Danny scrunches his hands into fists and makes himself yell. "Get the hell out!" There's a pause as they stare each other down. "Now!"

His mother flinches and leaves without a word, and Danny slams the door behind her. He sits back down at his desk and puts his head down again. He should be crying. He should be seething. He should be anything.

But he feels nothing. And as long as he's on this medication, he's always going to feel nothing.

CHAPTER TWO

"Hey, Jane. Watch out. You're gonna hit that—"

Slam!

Peter Davis's right leg whacks into the side of the water fountain and the wheelchair stops, but only for a moment.

"Oh. Sorry," Jane Scott says, her voice toneless. She pulls the chair back slightly, reconfigures the angle, and keeps pushing.

"That's okay," Peter forces himself to answer brightly. He squeezes his green eyes shut and has to swallow hard to keep his breakfast from coming up. He doesn't feel a thing. Someone has just driven his body forcibly into a large metal object and he doesn't feel so much as a twinge. Jane might as well have wheeled a sack of flour into the water fountain. Peter knows there must be a bruise forming on his knee, but he can't feel that, either. When is he going to get used to this?

"Academic Decathlon meet on Thursday . . . have to talk to Danny Chaiken about my audition piece . . . have

23

to get my application essays copied. . . . When can I do that? Okay, I can stop there before work. . . ."

Peter grips the arms of his chair as Jane pushes him through the crowded hallway toward the cafeteria. It's clear from her fairly constant muttering and the fact that innocent freshmen have to jump out of the way to keep from getting run over that she's not quite paying attention to what she's doing. He really doesn't want to be driven into anything else—inanimate or otherwise.

"So . . . sounds like you're pretty busy," Peter says, hoping to snap her back into the now so that she realizes he's kind of at her mercy.

There are a few moments of silence, and just as Peter's wondering if she heard him, she responds. "Yeah," she says. No elaboration.

Peter pushes himself up with his arms, shifting slightly in his chair so that his body is flush up against the left side. He tilts his head up and back so he can see her. He's always thought Jane is kind of pretty—in a stressed-out way. She doesn't wear much makeup, but with her big brown eyes, she doesn't really have to. And her light brown skin—just a tad darker than Peter's own—is always blemish free. Her black, shoulder-length hair is back today, and with her white button-down and the colorful scarf around her neck, she looks more like a teacher than a student. Of course, she doesn't look like much of anything from Peter's angle. He's got a great view of her chin and can actually see up her nose a bit. It's an odd way to suddenly have to look at people you've known all your life.

"So, do you know where you're going next year?" he asks, figuring this is a topic Jane will definitely be able to run with. All the brains love to talk about their future lives of academic triumph and intellectual brilliance. Not that he's friends with any of them, but he overhears them all the time, chattering away in homeroom about full rides to Duke and the injustice of the meal plan system at Harvard.

But Jane's face just gets hard, and Peter instinctively turns forward again, just in time to see Reed Frasier holding the door to the cafeteria open so that Jane and Peter can get through.

"Thanks," Peter says. Jane, still distracted, doesn't say anything.

"No problem," Reed answers.

Jane remains silent as she navigates through the tables and chairs, and Peter knows he's brought up a sore topic. But how could college be a sore topic with Falls High's number-one prodigy? As curious as he is, Peter isn't about to ask any more questions. It's none of his business. And he doesn't want to find out if the air between them can get any colder.

Jane wheels Peter over to the head of the table where his friends are already sitting and walks away without so much as a good-bye. *Well . . .* that *was fun,* Peter thinks sarcastically as he pulls his brown-bag lunch out of the side pocket on his chair.

"So, what's it like to have to spend so much time with Miss Stick-up-her-butt?" Keith Kleiner asks the second Jane is out of earshot. He takes a bite out of his egg salad sandwich and Peter starts to look away. But before he can, a big gob of egg hits the table and sits there among a few other blobs just like it. Keith could definitely win an award for gross eating habits.

"She's not that bad," Peter says, scratching an itch on the top of his shaved head. Even though she pretty much couldn't have been more rude to him, Peter feels kind of bad for Jane. The girl is obviously so stressed, she's blown a gasket somewhere. Why else would she be muttering her stream of consciousness aloud?

"Whatever," Max Kang says, flicking his greasy black hair away from his eyes. "That girl is definitely a candidate for stick-removal surgery."

The other guys all laugh at Max's lame joke, but Doug Anderson keeps laughing long after the others have returned to their soggy sandwiches and tiny little bags of chips. His blue-for-the-moment hair shakes as he holds his hand over his stomach and guffaws. Peter's mind suddenly flashes on an image of Cookie Monster and he smirks.

"Stoned?" he asks his other friends, raising his eyebrows.

"Very," Max and Keith answer in unison.

Finally Doug's laughing spree comes to a chuckling close and he looks up at Peter, a wide grin on his face, his brown eyes hardly focusing. Doug definitely deserves a good mocking if he thinks he's not going to be snagged, and Peter opens his mouth to give it to him, but Doug beats him to the punch.

"So, man, when are you gonna get out of that thing so we can go out and have some real fun?"

Peter's dig dies on his tongue and no one moves. It's as if someone freeze-framed their table in the middle of the laughing, screeching, bustling cafeteria. Max shoves Doug's massive shoulder and Doug is thrown off balance, leaning into the empty chair next to him—a testament to just how stoned he is, since he's about twice Max's size and has ten times his strength.

"What?" Doug blurts out, glaring angrily at Max.

"Shut *up!*" Max snaps.

Peter's heart is pounding sickeningly. Any second now the pity party is going to start up again, and he can't take that. He wishes he could just get up out of his chair right now and shock them all. It would be so great—like a scene out of a bad soap opera or something.

His mind suddenly flashes back to the other day, when he was alone in his room and felt what he now refers to in his thoughts as "the warmth." The odd, comforting, calming feeling that had come over him when he'd tried to move his legs and failed. When he'd been on the verge of breaking down and giving up. At that moment, he'd felt like everything was going to be okay.

And if that was true, maybe there was a chance. Maybe one day he *would* get out of this freakin' contraption and shut everyone up. Pull the plug on the pity party for good.

Peter looks up at his friends, who are all trying not to look at him. He imagines himself telling them about the warmth. Then he imagines them all cracking up laughing. There's no way they would take him seriously. He knows that if someone told him about something like that and he'd never experienced it, he'd think they were pretty much wacko. But Peter has to do something to break the silence or they're never going to make it through the remaining thirty-nine minutes of their lunch period.

"Don't worry about it," he says, nonchalantly pulling his food out of the crumpled brown bag. "I'll be raising hell with you guys again by the end of the year." He obviously doesn't know this for sure—far from it. But it has the desired effect. He feels each of their heads snap up and three pairs of eyes focus on him.

"How do you know that?" Max asks.

Peter shrugs. "I just do," he says.

At this, Doug lets out a scoffing exhale and leans his elbows on the table. "Whatever, dude. Don't go all psychic on us." He waggles his fingers in the air in the universal sign for anything associated with cosmic powers.

Peter feels his face heat up, and he stares down at his

food, now wishing that he could get up just for the freedom of being able to walk away from the table.

Sometimes his friends can really be annoying.

• • •

Monday evening, Meena sits on the floor in her room, her back up against the wooden chest at the foot of her bed. She's wearing fuzzy sweatpants, her old soccer sweatshirt, and a pair of heavy socks, but she can still feel the goose bumps on her skin—all the tiny little hairs on her arms are standing up. Her windows are wide open, the curtains billowing in the harsh breeze. It's thirty degrees outside, but Meena won't close the windows. She can't. If she does, she'll miss it.

Sappy *7th Heaven* is playing at a low volume on her TV. She can barely hear what the righteous father and innocent wide-eyed kids are saying, but she knows the drill. The kids are telling him everything about their uncontroversial little lives, and he's forgiving all of their shortcomings in one loving breath. Meena loves this show with a hateful passion.

A car turns onto the street outside and Meena's heart stops. She grabs the remote from the floor at her side and hits the mute button, even though the TV was barely making any noise at all. Her fingernails dig into the carpeting until the car drives by, the headlights flashing a beam across her bedroom wall.

There's a knock at her door and Meena jumps up. She

flies to the window, her heart frantically pounding. But one look out at the drive below tells her she's fine. Steven's car isn't there, so it's not him at her door. Meena is just sighing her relief when the doorknob turns and clicks, then turns and clicks again.

Another knock. "Meena?" It's her mother. "Why is this locked?"

Meena crosses the room and opens the door wordlessly. Both her parents walk in, her father fixing his gaze on her face as her mother quickly looks around the room as if she's expecting to find a boy or a bottle or a joint. She blinks a few times when she sees what her daughter is watching.

"It's freezing in here," she says, crossing to the windows.

"Don't!" Meena says loudly as her mom reaches to close them.

"Meena, I won't have you sitting in an icebox all night." She pulls the windows down but leaves them each open a crack. A moped flies by outside and Meena un-clenches her hands. She can still hear the road.

"Well, there's no point in beating around the bush here, sweetie," her father says, putting his hands in the pockets of his slacks. "You're going to start seeing a psychiatrist."

"What?" Meena blurts out, her mind racing. They're going to send her to a *stranger* to talk about her problems? What good could that possibly do? "There's no way I'm going to—" But Meena stops talking abruptly. Another car has turned onto the street and it's slowing down.

"You have to talk to someone, Meena. And you obviously won't talk to us. This behavior is just not normal. . . ."

The car pulls into the driveway. Squeaks. The engine dies.

"We don't understand why you lied about starting the fire. Why would you want everyone to believe . . ."

Footsteps on the walk. The front door opens and closes.

"And you dropped off the swim team and out of all of your clubs. . . ."

The creak of the stairs as he climbs.

"And you used to be on the phone with your friends till all hours. . . ."

And then he's there. Standing outside her room in the hallway. Standing outside *her* room in *her* house. She locks eyes with him over her father's shoulder. Tries to glare. He gazes right back. His eyes are soft, like he wants to comfort her. All sympathy. There's a small smile on his lips. There's no air in the room.

Then her father glances over his shoulder to see what she's looking at. "Steven," he says. "I didn't hear you come up."

"Everything okay?" Steven asks.

"Actually, this is a bit of a family matter," her father says apologetically.

Don't apologize to him, Meena thinks. *If you only knew . . .*

"Oh, I understand," Steven says, glancing at Meena again. "I'll get out of your way." Then he moves off down the hall.

When Meena returns her gaze to her mother's face, her vision is blurry with hot tears.

"Don't cry, Meena. It's going to be okay," her mother says. She reaches out with one hand, but Meena pulls back, hugging herself.

Her mother looks stricken and arranges her face into a stern expression. "Are you going to say anything?"

"Yeah," Meena says. There's a full-family hug taking place on the TV. "Could you please leave?"

Her mother sighs and looks at her father. They turn to go and Meena watches them walk out into the hallway. Steven may be gone, but she can still see him standing there, feel him looking at her. Meena follows her parents to the door and closes it behind them, turning the lock as quietly as possible. Then she closes the windows and locks them, too. She pulls down the blinds, turns off the TV, and sits on the edge of her bed, listening. He's out there. Waiting. She can wait, too. She can stay up all night if she has to.

• • •

"Ahhh . . . that was good," Jeremy says, finishing off the last bite of spicy shrimp from a Chinese food take-out box. He's ridiculously full—a sensation he happens to love. Taking a deep breath, he leans back in his father's rickety wooden desk chair so far that he almost falls over backward and has to grab the edge of the table for support.

His parents laugh as he catches his breath and steadies himself, and his little sister, Emily, rolls her eyes, smiling.

"You know you're not supposed to lean back in that chair," Emily says, sounding eerily like their mother. She flicks her red braids behind her back and shakes her head like Jeremy is just *so* immature.

Jeremy smiles. Damn, he loves his sister—her and her little Powerpuff Girls T-shirt. And he loves his parents and the way they look at each other across the table like they're high school sweethearts and not people who have been married for twenty years. And he loves these late night takeout dinners in his dad's office that they have at least once a week when his father can't seem to make himself leave the halfway house he owns and supervises. This is what life is all about. These silly little traditions. His mockably close family. Normalcy.

Someone walks past the open door to the office and Jeremy's heart hits his throat—not the best feeling when you've eaten as much as Jeremy just has. But it's only Tracy—one of the tenants of the halfway house, who sweeps up each night as her daily task. Jeremy sits back again, carefully this time, and tells himself to relax. If he keeps having a heart attack every time someone moves in this building, he'll be dead before he gets to his fortune cookie. He wishes someone would just *tell* him whether or not Josh is working so he could stop freaking out about the possibility of seeing him.

Emily looks up at their father. "Hey, is Josh here tonight?"

Jeremy stares at her. What is she, clairvoyant now?

"I want to show him my new backpack," Emily says, grinning. "Josh *loves* the Powerpuff Girls." She says this with a scathing glance at Jeremy, like he's a lesser man for not indulging her in her cartoon obsession the way Josh does.

"Hey! *I* love your backpack," Jeremy protests.

"Yeah, right," Emily says, laughing. "Then why did you try to make me buy the Superman one?"

"Because Superman could kick the Powerpuff Girls' butts," Jeremy says matter-of-factly.

"He could not!" Emily argues, tossing an unused spoon at Jeremy's head.

Jeremy's about to retaliate with a packet of sweet-and-sour sauce when their mother lifts her hands. "Not tonight!" she says. "I'm too tired to clean up after you two again!"

"I'll get you later," Jeremy promises, grinning.

"Yeah, whatever," Emily says, grinning back.

"To answer your question, Emily, Josh called in sick today," Jeremy's father says, leaning his elbows on the wooden tabletop.

Jeremy tries not to look affected by this last statement as his sister's face falls. But inside, he's reeling. *Is Josh really sick, or did he just call in sick because he doesn't want to see me?* Jeremy wonders. *Maybe he regrets kissing me.* What if

Josh is staying away, buying time to think of a way to let Jeremy down easy?

Well, he doesn't have to worry about it, Jeremy thinks defensively. *He won't be letting me down because it's not like I want to be with* him. Actually, the thought that Josh might not want him should be comforting. It is, in fact. This way he won't have to explain to Josh that he doesn't want to pursue anything with him. That he has a life. A girlfriend. A world that he'd like to keep intact.

And besides, it's not like I'm gay, Jeremy thinks. He's a football player. He has a girlfriend. One kiss does not make him gay.

Then why did you kiss him back? a little voice in his head asks.

Suddenly the door flies open with a crash and Ceecee Williams, one of the on-and-off tenants of the halfway house, bursts into the room, a ball of kinetic energy obviously brought on by some crazy combo of drugs. Her eyes are red and wild and she's practically coming out of her skin. As Jeremy's parents stand, Jeremy jumps up from his seat and instinctively grabs Emily, pulling her into the corner behind their father.

"What the hell kind of a place do you think you're running around here?" Ceecee shouts, getting right up in Jeremy's dad's face. Emily clutches Jeremy's hand and he gives it a reassuring squeeze, even though he's petrified. He's struck by the imposing figure his father cuts. He's not all that tall, but with his wrestler's build, he's three times the size of this wisp of a woman. Still, she's so strung out, she could be dangerous enough to negate the size difference.

"Ceecee, just—"

"Don't tell me to *just!*" she screams, flinging her arm up. "Don't you tell me to—"

"Ceecee, what have you taken tonight?" Jeremy's mother asks, approaching the woman tentatively. Jeremy watches, frozen, wishing his mother would back off. She suddenly looks so small in her sleek black suit and heels. What if Ceecee attacks her?

"I ain't takin' nothin'!" Ceecee screams, turning her crazed eyes on Jeremy's mother. "You so perfect! You always think I'm takin' somethin'!"

She lunges toward Jeremy's mother, but before she gets an inch, Jeremy's father grabs her from behind and holds her arms down. He's so quick and strong, there isn't even a struggle.

"Where are the kids, Cease?" his dad asks quietly. "Where are Tanya and John Jr.?"

Ceecee's head hangs and she instantly starts to cry, her kinky curls bouncing around her face. "They're home," she says, looking up at Jeremy's mother. "I think they're home. I didn't mean to leave 'em. I didn't mean to. I didn't."

Jeremy takes a deep breath as his mother steps forward and wraps her arms around Ceecee. She glances at Jeremy's father as she leads the weeping woman out of the room and Jeremy's dad nods. His parents are always doing this—communicating with simple gestures and looks. When his mother and Ceecee are out the door, Jeremy finally releases his grip on Emily's hand, but he feels like his heart won't stop pounding for days.

"Is Mom going to be okay with her?" Jeremy asks, taking a tentative step away from the corner—he's not sure if his legs are going to collapse or not. Emily runs across the room and wraps her arms around her dad's waist.

"They'll be fine," Jeremy's dad says, sighing. He runs his hand over Emily's hair as she clings to him and looks down at her with an apologetic smile. "Sorry about that, kids. I guess that's just the nature of the business."

"What's wrong with her?" Emily asks. She rests her chin on her father's stomach so she can look up and see his face.

"She's got a lot of problems, unfortunately," Jeremy's father says. "A lot of drug use. Her husband left her—"

"Yeah, but hasn't she been in and out of treatment like ten times?" Jeremy asks, leaning into the back of the folding chair his mother had been sitting in. "She has kids. How can she not be trying harder to get better?"

Jeremy's father gives him a hard look and he knows he's said something wrong. "*Three* times, Jeremy. And you have no idea what that woman has been through or what it takes to get over an addiction."

"Sorry, Dad," Jeremy says, feeling that hard ache he

gets in his chest whenever he feels he's let his father down.

His dad sighs again and gently pulls Emily's arms away from his waist. He sits down in his chair and nudges her onto his lap, where she sits sideways on one leg and leans her side into her father's chest.

"I'm sorry I snapped," he says to Jeremy. "It's just that I want you to know that every person deserves your compassion and respect. It takes all kinds of people to make up this world, and it's our job to try to understand them and accept them and do what we can to help."

Jeremy nods, looking down at the mess of boxes, plates, and plastic utensils on the table. He's heard this speech a million times before, and each time he hears it, he's reminded of what amazing people his parents are and how proud he is of them. The way they handled Ceecee . . . He knows he never could have been that calm and rational.

As he starts to clear the table, he can't stop thinking about what his father said about Ceecee and everything she's been through. It makes him feel like a whiny child. His problems are minuscule compared to what some people go through—especially since he has control over them. It was just one kiss. One kiss that could either completely complicate his life or mean nothing at all. It's up to Jeremy.

At that moment Jeremy resolves to forget about it for good this time. The next time he sees Josh, he'll act like nothing happened. And if Josh brings it up, Jeremy will tell him, point-blank, that it was a fluke. That he doesn't want to be with a guy. He likes his life the way it is.

And besides, Josh is probably not interested, anyway.

• • •

As Karyn turns her green VW convertible onto her block on Monday evening, the streetlights all flick on at once, causing her to suddenly feel like she's landing on a runway. Karyn glances up at the cloudy sky and sighs. Already dark. Practice has just ended and it's already dark. This is the one bad thing about fall. The night stretches out before her like a never-ending void. It's always the same. Shower, dinner—most likely alone—an hour of TV, an hour of attempting to concentrate on homework, a couple of hours on the phone, then bed. Life after school is seriously boring.

Karyn pulls into her driveway and slams on the brakes. Once again, her mother has parked right in the center of the driveway—not enough room for Karyn to park next to her and barely enough room for her to park behind. Sometimes she wonders if her mother forgets that she has a daughter she shares her house with—if she's genuinely surprised when Karyn walks through the front door every night. Karyn kills the engine, gets out, and walks around behind the VW. Her back bumper is hanging out over the sidewalk.

"Great!" Karyn says under her breath. She pulls her gym bag and backpack out of the passenger seat and slams the door. By the time she gets into the house, she's seething. When she sees her mother standing in front of the hall mirror, makeup caked on, hair sprayed, skirt hiked up, she sees red.

"Hot date?" Karyn demands, dropping her bags on the floor with a thud.

"Kind of," her mother says, smiling to herself. She doesn't even look at Karyn. Probably doesn't even notice her sarcasm.

"Perfect. Guess it's Lean Cuisine for me once again," Karyn says, stalking past her mother on the way to the kitchen at the back of the house. As she passes by, she catches her mother's eye in the mirror and they give each other the exact same narrow-eyed look.

"Don't take that tone with me, young lady," Karyn's mother snaps, dropping her eyeliner on the table and following Karyn into the kitchen.

Karyn flings open the freezer door and starts pawing through the dozen or so white-and-orange boxes, not really even looking at them. She's so angry, she probably couldn't read if she wanted to. And she's definitely not hungry. This just gives her something to do with her hands to keep them from strangling her mother.

"God, Mom, do you even hear yourself?" Karyn says, slamming the freezer door shut. A few of her mother's magnets clatter to the floor and ricochet across the room. "You sound like a bad Lifetime movie."

"Look, Karyn, I didn't want to get into this before my date, but your behavior leaves me no choice," Karyn's mom says, tossing her blond hair behind her shoulders in a manner that makes Karyn think of Jeannie. Her mother has the mannerisms of a teenager. It makes Karyn sick. She wonders if her mother decided to become a guidance counselor just so she'd never have to leave high school.

"Didn't want to get into what, Mom?" Karyn says, crossing her arms over her denim jacket and looking her mother directly in the eye. As if she can *see* her eyes under all that mascara.

"I know you think you've got it great with a mother who doesn't watch your every move and enforce curfews and check your breath when you come home, but you're starting to take advantage of my understanding, and it ends here."

A laugh bubbles up in Karyn's throat. Is she serious? She actually believes that Karyn thinks she has it great? Yeah, she really loves the fact that her mother goes out on dates every night and is never *there* to check her breath or enforce a curfew or keep an eye on her. Karyn feels like the luckiest girl on earth to have a slut for a mother.

Her tongue is itching to say all of this—*any* of this—but she knows she won't. Instead she does the usual. Takes the defensive.

"What are you talking about?" Karyn asks, not moving a muscle.

41

"I'm talking about the fact that you came home at 1 A.M. on Saturday," her mother says, shifting her hands to her hips. "I'm talking about the fact that you have no respect for me or this household, and that's going to change."

"Wait a minute, how do you know what time I came home on Saturday night?" Karyn asks. "You weren't even here."

Karyn remembers this distinctly because when Reed had dropped her off, he'd asked where her mother's car was. And Karyn had had to make up a story about the Taurus being in the shop so he wouldn't know that her mother was off sleeping with some guy Karyn had never even met but who sounded quite a bit like Regis Philbin on the answering machine. Reed knows a lot about her life, but he doesn't need *all* the gory details.

Karyn's mother blinks, and Karyn knows that she's struck some kind of nerve. "Mrs. Gillus told me," Karyn's mother says. "She said some guy dropped you off. And that you were sitting in the car for over an hour with the lights out."

Karyn feels her face flush all the way to the tips of her ears. Right. She and Reed sat in the car for an hour because they were *talking*, but she's not about to explain that to her mother.

"You've got the *neighbors* spying on me?" she shouts. It feels like the veins in her forehead are going to pop open.

"I didn't ask her to—"

"And if you're so upset about me coming home late on

42

Saturday night, then why did you wait until *Monday* to tell me?" Karyn spits out. "Is it because you've been so busy with this new dork *Barry* that you didn't want to bother dealing with me until I pissed you off?"

"Karyn!" her mother shouts. "You will not speak to me that way!"

Karyn pulls herself up straight and glares at her mother. This woman who could be her twin for all the creams, treatments, and masks she religiously applies to her face to make herself look younger.

"You can't tell me what I can and can't say. And maybe you can lecture me on being responsible when *you* learn the meaning of the word," Karyn says. She brushes past her mother before she can respond and heads back to the front door to get her bags. She can feel her mother following her and she keeps talking so that her mother can't. "You know, I think it's really hysterical that you're a *guidance counselor*," she says, hoisting her bags onto her shoulder. "You go to my school every day and tell random people how to live their lives; meanwhile, you go through guys like they're coming out of a Pez dispenser. I wonder what those kids' parents would think if they knew someone like you was telling their kids what to do."

A quick glance reveals that her mother's face is stricken, but Karyn won't allow herself to think about it. Let her mother be hurt. She's tired of being the only one that feels bad around here.

Karyn starts up the stairs and is not remotely surprised when her mother yells after her that she's grounded. She doesn't bother to remind her mother that she was *already* grounded, well before the horror of the 1 A.M. arrival. The woman is so self-involved, she can't even remember the punishments she doles out, let alone enforce them. Karyn slams the door to her bedroom and flings her heavy bags across her bed. They land on the floor on the other side, taking the magazines that had been strewn across her bedspread with them.

She grabs her phone and sits down hard on the floor, leaning her back up against her box spring. Her thumb automatically hits the speed dial button, then the number two.

"Pick up!" she says as the third ring sounds in her ear. "Come on, pick up." Karyn presses her fingertips into her forehead. She's near tears, and she takes a deep breath to keep them at bay. She will not cry over her mother.

"Hey, this is Reed! You know what to do after the beep, so—" The beep is piercing.

"Hey, it's me," Karyn says. "I really need to talk to you so . . . call me back."

She hangs up the phone and her foot starts to bounce uncontrollably. She stares at the little gray numbers on the handset and considers hitting the first speed dial button to call T. J. But what would be the point? He's always busy and she doesn't want to interrupt his studying with yet another sob story about her mother. Besides, T. J. has never been very good on the phone. He means well, but he often doesn't know what to say. He's better in person when he can hug her, hold her, make her feel like everything is going to be okay. But he's not here now. And wishing he was here just makes Karyn feel worse.

She grabs her stereo remote and turns on the CD player. A nice, loud, bass-heavy Destiny's Child song comes pounding through her speakers and Karyn leans her head back into the side of her mattress, closing her eyes. This is good. This will drown out everything else. She'll just sit here and breathe until her mother leaves. Then she can get on with the rest of her boring, pointless night.

CHAPTER THREE

Jeremy strides into school on Tuesday morning feeling good. More than good. He feels like he's gotten a new lease on life. The whole thing with Josh has just made him appreciate everything he has even more—everything that could be at risk if anyone ever finds out that he kissed a guy. He tugs down the sleeves of his varsity jacket as he turns down the main hallway, heading for the stairs so he can get to Tara's locker. All he wants to do right now is find her and plant a huge kiss on her lips. Then he knows everything will be fine.

"Hey, Jeremy!" Lainie Cruz says as she walks by with a few of her friends. "Tara's looking for you. Something about Halloween costumes."

"Thanks," Jeremy says with a smile. Leave it to Tara. When she gets her mind on something, she doesn't let it drop until she has an answer. Last night she left him a five-minute-long message rambling about the three coupley costumes she's come up with for them to wear to Mike

Chumsky's party this weekend. Jeremy can just envision them now, walking in hand in hand, wearing something perfect like Romeo and Juliet or Superman and Lois Lane or Buffy and Angel. Yeah, this is what he wants. Coupledom. Normalcy. Acceptance.

Everything he's worked so hard for since the day he first set foot in this school three years ago.

Jeremy is about to push through the doors to the stairwell when someone calls his name in a stage whisper. He turns around and is surprised to find Jane Scott, of all people, standing at the doorway to the library and motioning him over with her hand.

Jeremy cuts through the bustling hallway and stands in front of her, wondering what she could possibly be desperate to talk to him about. He talks to her now and then when she and Reed are working together at TCBY and he stops in for free yogurt, but they don't really move in the same circles. At least, they haven't in a very long time.

"What's up?" Jeremy asks, shoving his hands into the pockets of his jacket.

"You'd better see this," Jane says. With that, she turns and hurries back into the library. Still baffled, Jeremy slowly follows. Jane stops in front of a computer console and pulls up Ears, the school's unsanctioned gossip site. She steps back from the desk and crosses her arms over the front of her blue sweater, watching him intently.

Humoring her, even though he's pretty sure she's insane at this point, Jeremy leans down to read the screen. What he sees there makes all the blood in his body rush to his head.

Football Star Punting for the Other Team.

The headline runs above Jeremy's yearbook picture from last year and a story detailing the kiss. *The* kiss. Jeremy's vision seems to be rapidly clouding over, but he can make out a few choice phrases.

Half of Falls High's cutest couple . . .

Saturday night scandal . . .

Up against a wall . . .

Lips locked with a hot Kennedy guy . . .

Jeremy drops into a chair. He can't stop staring at the screen. He can't breathe. He keeps seeing Tara, his parents, his sister, his friends. Is this what it is to have your life flash before your eyes?

"I just thought you should know," Jane says tentatively. Her voice seems like it's right inside his head. "I don't care whether it's true or not. I just thought you should know in case people start acting weird or in case Tara asks about it. You know."

Jeremy feels himself nod. Hears himself say, "Thanks. You didn't have to . . . so . . . thanks." Jane's a good person for warning him. Most people would have stood back and watched what will most likely be a tabloid-worthy aftermath. He squeezes his eyes shut and holds his head in his hands. He's vaguely aware of Jane gathering her things and leaving the room. Vaguely aware of the bell ringing.

Finally, after at least ten minutes of catatonia, Jeremy forces himself to read the whole article. Twice. Josh is un-named, but it's bad. Really, really bad. Every other detail is right on. Someone had stood there and watched. Jeremy feels violated. Disgusted.

It didn't mean anything! his brain screams. *Don't they even care that it didn't mean anything? I love Tara. I don't want this.*

How could anyone have written this? They had to know it was going to ruin him.

And that's what's going to happen, Jeremy can feel it. Just sitting there, staring at the screen, he can already feel it starting to happen. He feels naked. On display. Totally exposed. And no one has even said anything to him yet. But they will. And once they start talking, they're never going to stop. Jeremy's whole world is about to fall apart.

And there's nothing he can do to stop it.

• • •

"Okay, what do I need, what do I need?" Karyn whispers to herself as she stares at the stack of books in the top section of her locker. Every morning she forgets something else. She gets to physics and has her history notebook, or she gets to English and has only her physics text. It never fails. She pulls out her ridiculously heavy math textbook and dumps it into her backpack. She's sure she's going to

49

have scoliosis by the end of this year from carrying it around.

"Karyn!"

Her heart jumps in surprise at the sound of her name. Before she's even sure who's calling her, she presses her lips together and checks her eyeliner in her locker mirror. It's all force of habit, these little adjustments. She's never worn too much makeup, but she's been a constant primper ever since she got her first subscription to *Seventeen* in sixth grade. Out of the corner of her eye she sees Reed jogging toward her, the crowd in the hall parting for him automatically.

"Hey," Reed says, leaning his shoulder against the locker a couple of doors down from hers. He takes off his battered Yankees cap, runs his hand over his shaggy red hair, and replaces the hat, curling the brim in one, swift, unconscious motion. He's all flushed, and when his hat was off, Karyn noticed that the hair over his forehead was curled with sweat. The fact that he probably ran here all the way from the far end of the parking lot where he always parks his Subaru is not lost on Karyn.

"Are you okay? I wanted to call you back last night, but I got home so late. . . . There was this freak syrup accident at work and I had to clean it up and I didn't get out of there until after eleven."

"Freak syrup accident?" Karyn says, amused. She knows he wants to talk about the pathetic message she left

50

on his machine last night, but she definitely doesn't, so she decides to keep it light.

"Yeah, the new guy put a two-gallon container of chocolate syrup back in the cabinet upside down and it leaked all over the place and I . . ." He pauses, winded, and catches his breath. "Forget it. What happened?" he asks. The freckles on his nose make him look younger than his seventeen years, which makes the concern that lines his face that much sweeter.

"Nothing. I'm sorry I freaked you out," Karyn says. "It was just my mom . . . you know . . . the usual psychotic-ness." Her face flushes a bit under the scrutiny of Reed's gaze. He's studying her, trying to see if she's brushing off something too big and messy to be brushed. But she really had felt a lot better this morning, just like she always does after a big blowout with her mother. Nothing's ever going to change, so why let it ruin her day? As always, her mother had still been asleep when Karyn got in the shower, and when Karyn had left, her mother had been in the shower. They hadn't even had to see each other. And now that Karyn is in a better mood, she doesn't want to dredge it all up again.

"Are you sure?" Reed asks. He starts to lift his hand, and for a split second Karyn's heart stops. She's sure he's going to touch her shoulder or brush her hair away from her face and she feels a charge sizzle through the air at the idea of the intimacy of such a gesture. But then he pulls back and tucks his hands under his arms. It all happens so quickly, Karyn can't be sure if it actually happened at all. "Uh . . . you sounded really out of it on the phone," Reed says.

"Yeah, I just wanted to vent," Karyn replies. She zips up her bag and slams her locker door. "I'm better today."

Reed smiles and they start down the hall together toward their homerooms. "Well, it's too bad that you're so okay, because I was going to suggest a little meatball-hero therapy at lunch."

Karyn grins and her stomach grumbles even though it's only ten minutes after eight. Way too early to be thinking about tomato sauce and red meat. "Phil's?" she says, grabbing the leather arm of his varsity jacket.

"That's what I was thinking," Reed says, tilting his head as he shrugs it off. "But if you don't need a superspicy pick-me-up . . ."

"I'm in!" Karyn says. She loves the fact that Reed not only knows her favorite greasy-food dive, but her usual order. "One can never have enough meatball therapy."

They stop in front of the door to her homeroom and Reed smiles down at her. "I'll meet you at your car at twelve-forty sharp."

"Got it," Karyn says. "Oh, wait!" she says, bringing her hands to her forehead as he starts to walk away. "I forgot. I'm supposed to get the chemistry notes from Amy at lunch. I need to copy them before class this afternoon. I kind of spaced during class yesterday."

"That's understandable," Reed says, lifting one shoulder. "After all, Mr. Therber is the single most boring man on the planet." Karyn laughs at his deadpan humor and Reed smiles. "So we'll bring the heros back from Phil's and eat here. You get your meatball therapy with a side of chem."

"Sounds like a plan," Karyn says.

As Reed walks off toward his classroom, she watches him go, shaking her head at the little klatch of junior girls who follow him with their eyes, blatantly salivating. When he ducks into his room, the girls all turn to look at Karyn and she raises her eyebrows at them. They know that she knows what they're thinking, so they all try to look nonchalant—like they all glanced over at her at the same exact time out of sheer coincidence. She knows they're speculating about her and Reed and wondering if they really are just friends. Unbelievable. They see two people who are close and immediately assume they're together. And they probably all hate her because they all want Reed. Jealousy is the easiest thing to spot on another teenage girl.

Meanwhile, all they see in Reed is a hottie athlete. Not that he's not hot. But Karyn feels lucky to be one of the few who knows that he's also basically the greatest guy on earth. And he's *her* best friend.

Huh, Karyn thinks, smirking as she strides into homeroom. *They* should *be jealous*.

"Seriously man, I'm not even kidding you, it's about four hundred degrees in Mr. Dayne's room, right? And we're all, like, *dying*," Danny tells Keith Kleiner, Max Kang, and Cori Lerner as they hang by the vending machines between classes. "The radiator's broken and you can, like, *hear* the steam hissing out. It was insane."

"So whadya do, dude, take your shirt off or something?" Keith asks. He and Max look at each other and Keith lets out his hyenalike laugh, whacking Max's meaty chest with the back of his hand while Max, ever the stoic, merely acknowledges Keith's not so creative joke with a vague smile.

Cori simply looks at Danny and rolls her eyes at the other guys' antics, flicking a lock of hair off her forehead. Danny feels himself start to blush, loving the fact that Cori just shared a private moment with him.

He pops the top on his Mountain Dew and sucks down about half the contents in one swallow. Someone once told him the stuff makes people really hyper, and he could use a jolt right now. He'd been out of it enough before Dayne's class, but the heat in there had almost put him right to sleep.

"No, man, I'm trying to *tell* you," Danny says, attempting to maintain this high level of animation, even though he feels like he could basically lie down on the floor and take a nap right now. Another lovely side effect of the new drugs his shrink has put him on. Constant exhaustion!

"Mr. Dayne is writing this problem on the board and he keeps wiping at his forehead, ya know, with a paper towel. And then he turns around, and I'm not even kidding, his rug is about an inch farther back on his head than it's supposed to be."

"No way," Keith says, his dark eyes wide as he chews, openmouthed, on a PayDay bar.

"Seriously. And we all noticed it," Danny says.

"You're so full of it," Cori says with a laugh.

"Ask anyone!" Danny protests. "So anyway, all the girls are giggling and it's all I can do to keep from busting a gut, but then it gets worse." He brings his hand to his forehead, demonstrating Dayne's hairline, smiling at his friends' rapt attention. "It's inching back, bit by bit, and now you can *see* the glue. It was so nasty. I swear, by the end of class I thought the thing was just going to fall off the back of his head."

Max blows out a sigh. "That's brutal, man."

"The best part about it was that he didn't even notice," Danny says, laughing. "Dayne is such a moron."

"Danny!"

At the sound of his name uttered in a tense female voice, Danny freezes and looks at his friends. Is he in trouble? Is it that witch vice principal, Ms. Depiero, come to drag him off to detention for slamming a teacher? His friends don't look anything but surprised, so Danny turns around. Jane Scott hurries up to him, giving off the somehow frazzled yet calm and collected vibe she always does. It's like her whole body is moving at warp speed even though her face is placid and her gaze steady. The girl is a walking contradiction.

"Can I talk to you?" Jane asks, tapping her pen continuously on the cover of the notebook she's clutching while casting a dismissive glance at Max, Keith, and Cori.

"Yeah. What's up?" Danny says as he and Jane step a few feet away from the others.

"Ooh! Danny's making it with the valedictorian!" Keith singsongs like a fifth grader. Danny raises his hand, telling Keith to stuff it. Then he glances over his shoulder at Cori and shakes his head slightly as if to say, *"Yeah, like I'd ever date Jane."* It isn't like he thinks Cori is interested in him, but it wouldn't hurt to let her know that he is not, in fact, making it with the valedictorian.

Cori chuckles. Silent message: *"I know she's not your type."*

Danny smiles in relief.

"Just ignore them," Danny tells Jane.

"I was planning on it," Jane says coolly.

"Right," Danny says with a short laugh. He's always liked Jane, but sometimes she's just all business. Today she's wearing a blue cardigan sweater over a pristine white T-shirt and a pair of black cords with shiny black shoes. She looks like one of his mother's PTA buddies.

"So, here's the situation," Jane says. "I have to make an audition tape for the conservatories and Mr. Vega says it's best to have an original piece, basically to get their attention. I'm sure they hear the same pieces over and over again."

"Makes sense," Danny says, clueless as to where this conversation is going. Danny and Jane are in music theory and jazz band together, and they hang out in those groups, but he wouldn't say they're exactly *friends*. Why is she telling him about her application process?

"Well, I really liked that last piece you wrote for theory," Jane continues. "And since I don't have the time to write one myself, I was wondering if you could put something together for me?" She raises her eyebrows and looks at him hopefully, but it takes Danny a moment to process what she's saying. "I could pay you," Jane throws in.

"No, no, I wouldn't ask you to *pay* me," Danny says. He brings his hand to his forehead, suddenly having trouble focusing once again. "So let me get this straight," he says. "You want me to write your audition piece?" It comes out sounding kind of condescending and Danny can see it in the step-back expression that's come over Jane's dark features.

"Look, if you don't want to—"

"No! I do!" Danny says. He takes a deep breath and crosses his arms in front of his oversized T-shirt, pinching at his sides. "Really, I . . . thanks for asking," he says finally, sounding like a lameass but glad he's actually started making sense. "And you don't have to pay me. Really."

"Great! Thanks, Danny!" She glances at her watch and it's obvious her mind is already zeroing in on her next task. "I'll talk to you more about it in class, okay?"

"Cool," Danny says with a nod, trying to be nonchalant

as Jane walks away. Inside, however, he couldn't be more psyched. This could be exactly what he needs! He's totally flattered that Jane thought to ask him, and now that he has a real purpose for writing—a real goal and something at stake—maybe he'll be able to get something out. If he can just start writing again, he knows everything will be fine.

●●●

"Thanks, man," Peter says to the geeky freshman who's holding the door to the nurse's office open for him. He pushes at the wheels on his chair and jerks into the room, turning to face Nurse Meija, who's sitting behind her rather large desk. The door closes behind him and she looks up from the crossword puzzle she's working on.

"Hello, Peter," she says with her signature bright smile, causing her dark skin to crease in a million places. "Are we having another headache today?"

"Yeah," Peter says, trying not to cringe at her use of the word *we*. In the three-plus years that Peter has been attending this school, he's sure he's never heard Nurse Meija use the word *you*. It's always, "Are we really sick or are we just trying to get out of a test?" or, "Shall we call your mom and see if she'll come get us?"

What is that about?

"Can I get some Tylenol?" Peter asks, biting back the urge to ask if "we" can get some.

"No problem, sweetie," she says, turning to unlock the cabinet behind the desk.

Peter sits back in his chair and waits patiently for her to produce the little packet of pills. He's been in here a lot lately, doing just this. Ever since his accident, he's been getting more headaches than ever before. The doctors attribute it to stress. Being constantly stuck in his chair, Peter thinks boredom might also have a lot to do with it.

He sighs and looks left, glancing into the little room where students wait out upset stomachs, dizzy spells, and other ailments. From there they're either sent home, if Meija believes they're ill, or back to class, if she's unconvinced. The door is open and Peter starts when he sees Meena lying on the small bed inside, staring at the ceiling, with her arms flat at her sides. She looks like death. Her skin is pale and she's not moving a muscle, and it's way too easy for Peter to picture her lying just like that in a coffin.

"I'm going to have to get some from the back," Nurse Meija says, standing and smoothing down the front of her pink blouse. "I'll be back in a sec."

"'Kay," Peter says, tearing his eyes away from Meena.

Out of the corner of his eye, he sees Meena turn her head to look at him and he feels an unusually strong rush of relief. It's not like he actually thought she was dead, but it's nice to see her move.

As soon as Meija has disappeared down the little hall that leads to her supply room, Peter wheels himself a bit closer to the door.

"Hey," he says to Meena, folding his hands in his lap.

"Hey," she says. Her eyes are totally blank and it's disconcerting.

"So, are we feeling barfy or are we just trying to get out of a trig test?" Peter says, imitating Nurse Meija's high-pitched voice.

Meena cracks a small smile and Peter grins back, grateful that the blankness is gone.

"Little bit of both, I guess," she says. Then she turns her head, focusing once again on the ceiling.

Peter clears his throat and looks down at his lap, unsure of whether he should wheel away and leave her alone or stay there and keep talking. It's so hard to read people sometimes. But something tells him to stay put. Stay with her. Even if it's just for a minute.

"So, you've been getting headaches?" Meena says suddenly, surprising Peter.

"Yeah," he says, and shrugs. "You know."

"Me too," Meena says matter-of-factly. "Is it because of the accident?" she asks. Totally straightforward. No sympathy. No pity. No morbid curiosity. It's just a question. Unbelievable—the first just plain question he's been asked by anyone in so long.

"They think so," Peter says. He pushes his hands into his armrests, shifts in his seat. "What about yours?"

Meena blinks and Peter can swear he sees tears in her eyes. Then she takes a deep breath and as fast as they appeared, they're gone.

"Just stuff," she says. "You know."

She brings her hand to her forehead and Peter can see the fading scar from the burn she gave herself the week before at the diner. He swallows hard, remembering what it was like to watch her do that to herself. Watch her press the burning cigarette into her flesh like it was nothing.

Whatever kind of *stuff* Meena's talking about, Peter has a feeling it's not your average kind. Not the kind most of the kids in this school are worried about. He wants to ask her what it is. Wants to give her the chance to let it out. But he knows that's ridiculous. Meena has plenty of friends to talk to. Why would she want to talk to him?

"Found it!" Nurse Meija says, walking back into the room with a white box full of little pill packets.

"I guess I'll see you around," Peter says to Meena.

But her eyes are closed again, her breathing heavy. Just like that, Meena has fallen asleep.

• • •

Jeremy stares at the clock on the back wall of the library, watching the second hand as it ticks silently away. It's three minutes after nine, which means that at any moment the bell will ring, signaling the end of first period. He's missed homeroom. He's missed history. He's already screwed. He has to go to his next class or he'll be even more screwed.

But what's worse? Jeremy wonders. *Explaining to Ms. Depiero why I missed class or going out there and facing the entire student body? Facing Tara? Facing the team?*

The librarians haven't noticed him yet. As always, they are up at the front of the library behind the counter, doing nothing but looking perpetually annoyed. Maybe he can hide out in here all day. Maybe he can move in here and live among the stacks. It has to be better than the alternative.

"Okay, Mandile, get a grip," Jeremy whispers to himself, still watching the clock. "Lainie obviously doesn't know about this yet, or she wouldn't have been so normal this morning. So Tara can't know yet. Maybe if you get to her first . . ."

Yes. That's it. He'll find Tara and tell her he just saw the funniest thing on the gossip site. *"Where are they getting their stuff these days?"* he'll say. *"Are they just sitting around, thinking of the most absurd things possible and writing them down?"* That's it. It has to work. Forget everybody else. They can think whatever they want. Tara is the one who matters. Once everyone sees that she's still with him, they'll know the story isn't true.

Even though it is, the little voice in Jeremy's head reminds him.

Jeremy ignores it and stands up defiantly at the exact moment the bell rings. The librarians look up, surprised, when they hear his chair scrape back, but Jeremy is out the door before they can ask questions.

Holding his breath, Jeremy ducks into the rapidly filling hallway, then realizes he's hunkering guiltily and forces himself to stand up straight. His heart is slamming against his rib cage, but he keeps moving. He hazards a few glances at some random people, defying them with his eyes to say anything but praying they won't.

And they don't.

The farther Jeremy walks, the more amazed he is. No one says a word to him, except a few "hellos" and "what's ups?" No one is even looking at him funny. Jeremy feels the first tentative strands of relief rush through his body. Maybe no one has read the story yet. Maybe nobody knows!

Scanning the hallway now, Jeremy spots Naomi Kennedy, editor of *Ears*, up ahead and starts to jog, dodging and weaving between the little crowds of students who are wandering or rushing to their next classes.

"Naomi," he says quietly when he's within earshot.

She turns around and her blue eyes brighten behind her tortoiseshell glasses the moment she sees Jeremy. It's all he can do not to sock the smug smile right off her mousy little face.

Be cool, he tells himself. *If you don't act cool, she'll suspect something.*

He smiles back. Casually adjusts his backpack and leans one shoulder against the wall. He's all about unconcern.

"I guess you saw the story," Naomi says, cocking her head and flicking her eyes over Jeremy from head to toe like she's looking for signs of a breakdown. She's not going to get any.

"Yeah. Didn't know that *Ears* was specializing in fiction these days," Jeremy says. Perfect. Light. Joking. His heart is slamming again, though. Naomi just looks amused, not chagrined and embarrassed for getting caught in the act of printing lies.

That's because they're not lies, Jeremy's little voice says.

"So you're denying the story?" Naomi asks, leaning her shoulder against the wall so that she's facing him.

"I'm asking you to take it down," Jeremy says. He looks her directly in the eye, hoping for the remote possibility that she might be intimidated by him. He can be imposing if he wants to be.

"So you're *not* denying the story," she says, eyebrows raised.

"Of course I'm denying the story," Jeremy spits back. It comes out louder than he intends and a few girls who happen to be walking by look at him like he's lost it. Which he has.

Naomi grins. She's loving this. Once again Jeremy has the disconcerting urge to deck her. Doesn't she realize she's ruining his life?

"I'm not taking it down," she says prissily. "It's a gossip site, Jeremy. And you have to admit, it's *good* gossip." She starts off down the hall but turns and walks backward to wave at him and rub the salt a little bit deeper into his wound.

"But thanks for the quote!" she calls. "I can use that for tomorrow's article. Jeremy Mandile denies the story . . . vehemently."

The coy, cocky look in her eye tells Jeremy all he's done is confirm for her that the story is very much the truth.

CHAPTER FOUR

By the time Jeremy emerges from the lunch line on Tuesday afternoon, his back hurts from keeping it rigid all morning. He's been on the defensive all day, and during last period he noticed Donnie Giles and Katie Martino whispering and looking back at him every five seconds. No one has said anything to him yet, but that's sure to end the moment his friends find out. Whether they believe the story or not, they aren't going to let this one go.

As Jeremy crosses the crowded room to the table his friends normally sit at when they're not going off campus, he scans their faces to see if they seem to be discussing anything juicy. They all look normal—not intrigued or scandalized. Karyn and Reed are, as always, talking alone together at the end of the table, eating heros they obviously brought back from Phil's. Gemma and Carlos are playing tonsil hockey at the other end, and between them are a bunch of loudmouthed guys and girls eating and laughing it up. *Maybe they haven't read it or heard about it yet*, Jeremy hopes as he sinks into the empty chair between Karyn and Shaheem Dobi and diagonally across from Reed.

The table falls silent.

So maybe he was wrong.

"Fag," someone says under his breath. Raucous laughter ensues. Karyn tenses up next to Jeremy and glances at Reed, who does not look amused. Jeremy fights back the humiliated flush that wants to color his cheeks. He can't let this bother him. If he does, they'll all think it's true.

It is true.

"Just kidding, man," Mike Chumsky says, leaning forward so that Jeremy can see him past Shaheem's broad frame. Mike smiles and everyone else goes back to eating.

Jeremy takes a deep breath and looks down at the food he is definitely not going to have the stomach to eat. Well, that wasn't so bad. Could've been a lot worse.

"So . . . was he *cute?*" Mike asks in a singsongy voice. More laughter. Mike laughs louder than anyone else at his own humor, his mouth open to show the leftover bits of his last bite of macaroni and cheese.

"Mike, shut the hell up," Reed blurts out. He shoots Mike a don't-mess-with-me look. Mike stares back for a moment, obviously wanting to say something, but then thinks better of it and goes back to his lunch. In fact, everyone at the table is suddenly *very* interested in their food.

Jeremy's stomach turns over and over and he starts to

sweat. He's grateful to Reed for standing up for him, but it seems like if he thinks Jeremy needs defending, then he thinks Jeremy did it. The thought that Reed suspects the truth works away at Jeremy's mind faster than any comment Mike Chumsky could ever throw at him. The others all take their cues from Reed. The guy doesn't realize it, but they do. If *they* think that *Reed* thinks that Jeremy is gay, then they'll all believe it, too. Jeremy can feel all the blood rushing through his veins and clutches his hands together under the table to keep from shaking. He has to do something. He has to say something. He can't let this happen.

"Jeremy, are you okay?" Karyn asks discreetly, placing her hand on the back of his shoulder and tilting her head in concern.

"You guys want to know the truth?" Jeremy announces loudly, causing Karyn to jump and withdraw her hand. Everyone looks at him, and the morbid curiosity is blatant on their wide-eyed faces.

Reed leans forward slightly. "Jeremy, you don't have to—"

"No! I want to tell them what happened," Jeremy says, his eyes flashing. He is shaking now, and he's sure his face is bright red, but he ignores it. "I did go to a Kennedy party last weekend and some fag did kiss me."

I can't believe I did that, he thinks. *I can't believe I just used the word* fag.

Stunned silence. Jeremy keeps talking.

"But what the story *didn't* say is that I laid him out one second later," Jeremy asserts. Everyone is just staring at him, and he's not sure whether or not they believe him. All he can do is keep talking. "Little fairy hit the ground like a girl," he says, throwing in a strained laugh.

Jeremy feels Karyn pull away from him. "Tara and I have been dating for two years, man. I'm not gay," he says. "You guys know that."

For a few moments no one moves. No one chews. It seems like no one is even breathing. Jeremy knows he's made a misstep. His friends have never seen him lose it before. Jeremy is, in fact, known for his levelheadedness. For the millionth time that day, he wishes he could just disappear. Then Shaheem shifts in his seat and slaps Jeremy once on the back.

"Yeah, we know it, man," he says. He only looks at Jeremy for a split second.

"Not that there's anything wrong with that," Mike says loudly, doing his bad Seinfeld impression. There are a few relieved laughs and the conversation comes back to the table.

Jeremy feels uncomfortable in his own skin. Gemma and Lainie won't even look at him, and they both seem very pale. Jeremy glances at Karyn and she looks away. With a sinking disgust, he realizes that he may have just convinced them he wasn't "punting for the other team"— *may have* being the operative words—but now they all think he's a bigot.

Overwhelmed by shame, self-pity, embarrassment, and anger, Jeremy pushes away from the table, dumps his tray, and walks out of the school. For the first time all day, he doesn't care how it looks. All he wants to do is escape.

• • •

Doctor Lansky. Doctor . . . Lan . . . sky. Doctor Philip Lansky.

As Meena sits in the waiting room at her new shrink's office on Tuesday afternoon, she can't seem to stop repeating the guy's name in her head. She feels like it should mean something to her, the name of this person who's supposedly going to get her to open up, spill, bare her soul. The guy she's obviously not going to say a word to. If she tells him anything, he'll know. He'll know who she is . . . no . . . *what* she is. And he'll obviously tell her parents. She wonders if he'll tell them flat out that their daughter is a dirty slut or if he'll just state the facts and let them draw that conclusion for themselves.

Meena slumps down farther on the couch, the leather squeaking beneath her as she pulls up her legs and hugs them to her chest. Meena's mother is sitting next to her and she can see their reflection in the shiny glass of a framed poster across the way. Her mother gives her posture a reproachful glance, which Meena ignores. She's too busy wondering what she's supposed to talk about with this stranger for an hour when she can't talk about anything he's going to want her to talk about.

It's not like Meena doesn't *want* to talk to someone. Part of her knows that if she does—if she gets it all out— she'll have to feel at least somewhat better. Sometimes she feels like she's going to explode just from keeping it bottled up. But how can she talk to anyone when just being around people makes her uncomfortable?

You did feel comfortable once today, remember? the little voice in her mind whispers. *So comfortable, you even fell asleep.*

Meena's brow knits as she recalls the encounter with Peter Davis earlier that day. She hadn't slept all night and she'd been so tired this morning, she'd felt nauseous. So she'd gone to the nurse's office, but her mind had been racing so fast, she still hadn't been able to fall asleep. Not until Peter had been there by her side. What is it with Peter Davis lately? Why does he always have such a calming effect on her? First after the fire and now this. Why is he—

"Now remember, Meena," her mother says, interrupting her thoughts. "You can tell Dr. Lansky anything and everything that's bothering you. He's here to help."

And then Meena's thoughts are off and running again.

Everything, everything. He could tell my parents everything. Just the thought makes her want to bolt from the room and never look back. Meena glances at the door. Not a bad idea.

She sits up, considering the distance between herself

and the path to freedom—out that door, then out the door to the building—and wonders if anyone in the room would try to stop her. She's just assessing the potential strength of the stocky nurse behind the counter when another door opens and Danny Chaiken walks out.

Meena stares at Danny, jarred by the presence of one of her classmates. Up until that moment, she'd almost felt like she was in another universe. Danny is standing there, head tipped forward as he stares at the floor, hands tucked under his arms. An older man with a graying beard and salt-and-pepper hair speaks into Danny's ear in low tones and Danny nods as if his head is resting on a Slinky instead of his neck. It's clear all he wants to do is get away. Meena's stomach squeezes for him. She can't remember the last time she saw the normally confident, funny, hyperkinetic Danny look so vulnerable.

The talk ends and Danny finally lifts his face. His eyes immediately lock with Meena's and he looks sad . . . and defeated. In a flash, Meena does remember. She remembers the last time Danny looked like this. Seven years ago. On that day. That day she never ever thinks about.

Danny quickly looks away and without a word is out the door. Meena is vehemently jealous of him and of his freedom from this place.

"Meena Miller?"

Meena's mother instantly stands.

The gray man looks at Meena with a smile most grown-ups would probably think is welcoming. It makes Meena's skin crawl. "You can come in now," he says.

"Meena, get up," her mother says.

Standing, Meena hopes the pounding of her pulse isn't visible to the outside world. She doesn't want these people to know how freaked she is. The gray man reaches out his hand for Meena to shake as she crosses the room. Meena glances over her shoulder at her mother, who's still standing there clutching her bag and trying to look supportive. Meena can't help thinking she looks more like a helpless woman whose child is being cuffed and booked.

"I'm Dr. Lansky," the gray man says. "It's nice to meet you."

She just stares at his hand as she walks by him into his office. She hears the door close behind her, and now there are three doors between her and freedom.

"Have a seat," Dr. Lansky says, clearly unperturbed by the slight she gave him at the door.

Meena looks around. On one side of a wooden coffee table there's a comfy-looking, worn-in chair, clearly the doctor's. Across the table from that, there's a couch with a couple of throw pillows that looks equally worn, and to each side of the table are two more chairs—one straightbacked and leather, the other low and soft. Meena suddenly feels like this is a test. As if the doctor thinks that the chair she chooses will be the first window into her soul. She briefly wonders where Danny sat.

The soft chair looks like the most comfortable, but she doesn't know if she *wants* to get too comfortable, so she considers the high-backed chair, but she's not sure she can sit in that for an hour without squirming, so she thinks maybe the couch is the way to go, but that seems too laughable—going to the shrink and spreading out on a couch. It's so cliché. And then he'll probably think she's ready to talk, which she definitely is not, so maybe if she—

"Meena?"

Oh my God, I'm so stupid, Meena thinks. *I don't even know the right place to sit.*

She pulls her jacket tight around her and sits right smack in the middle of the couch.

Dr. Lansky settles into his chair, folds his hands on his stomach, and smiles. "So, tell me a little bit about yourself," he says.

Meena stares back. There's nothing to say. Ask her that question a few months ago and it would have been an easy, breezy answer. *Well, I'm on the swim team and the lacrosse team and I might win MVP, I love school and I want to study law someday, I have great friends. I love swimming and music but just the hard stuff—no *NSYNC for this girl. Things are generally great.*

But none of that's true anymore. She's nothing like she used to be. In fact, she's nothing much at all.

Meena swallows hard. "You don't want to know about me," she says. "No one does."

• • •

Tuesday evening, Peter slumps in his chair at the kitchen table, following his mother with his eyes. She still has her faded, light blue flowered oven mitts on as she brings the heavy platter of chicken Kiev to the table. The scent of melting cheese fills Peter's nostrils as wisps of steam roll up off the meat and into the air. Peter's stomach lets out a growl, but he frowns. Once again, his mom is serving up one of his favorite meals.

"This looks great, Laura," his father says as she finally sits down across from him at the table. They smile at each other and Peter rolls his eyes. Dinnertime has become a scene out of a 1950s newsreel about the close-knit nature of the perfect American family. What a joke.

Peter's dad reaches in front of him to pick up the serving spatula. He lifts one of the pieces of stuffed chicken off the platter, waits for the sauce to drip off, then plops it onto the dinner plate in front of Peter, who feels his face start to redden with embarrassed anger. This is another new thing—his dad serving him first. Like because his legs are nonfunctioning he is somehow no longer able to pass plates and dish up food.

Peter glances at his mom, who sits smiling at him in full-on June Cleaver mode, and feels like shouting at them to just be normal. Dinner has always been Peter's favorite time of the day. Even when he is royally pissed off at his parents for their complete lack of anything resembling involvement—with him, with each other, with the world in general—he can always commune with them over food. They are both amazing cooks, and the mood around the dinner table is always light, if noncommunicative. Usually Peter relishes the nice, shallow conversations he and his parents have over the meal. They're pretty much the only conversations that ever happen in his house.

But ever since his accident, dinner has taken on a new flavor. Not only have his parents been stuffing him with every heavy, saucy, meaty food imaginable, they've also been so oversolicitous of him, it makes him want to hurl. Not the best feeling to have at the dinner table.

"Peter? Are you going to eat?" his mother asks finally.

Neither of his parents has touched their meal yet. Another new habit—they're waiting for him to start first. Peter's skin prickles with anger. Enough is enough.

"Do you really think this is going to help?" he bites out.

Silence. His parents look at each other and he can hear their thoughts. *What do we do? He sounds angry. Maybe it's one of those traumatic experience aftermath symptoms. Just be calm.*

"Seriously," Peter says, shoving away his plate. It hits the platter, making a loud cracking noise. "You guys have been stuffing me with food like I'm getting set for the slaughter. Do you think if you get just enough gravy into me, I'm going to walk again?"

"Now, Peter," his father says, laying his hands flat on the table. "The doctors said—"

"I don't give a crap what the doctors said!" Peter shouts.

His mother flinches and his father just sits there. Peter's veins are practically bursting out of his skin and his eyes are tearing up and his parents are just sitting there. No one's asking him if he's okay. No one's asking him what's wrong. No one in this room cares what's going on in his head.

Peter takes a deep breath. Twists his napkin in his hands. Stares at his lap. "You guys haven't asked me once since I got home from the hospital . . . you haven't asked me what I'm thinking or . . . or how I feel."

He wraps the napkin tight around his index finger, turning the tip bright red as all the blood gathers under the nail. There's a bubble in Peter's throat and he knows that if it comes up, he's going to cry. He hasn't cried in front of his parents since he was ten. Since the day he turned ten, actually. He remembers it like it was yesterday. His mother hugged him, but his father walked away. He can remember what his father's back looked like when it turned on him. His father was so much bigger than him, it was like looking at a wall. The image has never left Peter.

Partially because of how devastating it felt at the time. Partially because his relationship with his father has never been the same since that day. The Saturdays playing

Frisbee in the backyard stopped. The yearly treks to Yankee Stadium stopped. Even the good-night hair musses stopped. And Peter knows why. Because of what happened that day. Because what happened was all Peter's fault. It's obvious that even his father blames him.

His mother clears her throat. "Well, honey, the doctors said not to pressure you into—"

"Screw this!" Peter says through clenched teeth. He swallows to keep the bubble down and shoves himself away from the table. It seems to take him forever to maneuver his chair around and get it out of the room, but no one tries to stop him. No one tries to call him back.

Peter clumsily bangs his way into his new bedroom and slams the door; then he just sits there, inches from it, seething. His parents are such clueless morons. Everything they say is recited directly from the pamphlets they received at the hospital. Colorful little trifolded papers with titles like "Coping with Paralysis" and "When a Loved One Hurts." They're saying everything they're supposed to say. But they can't seem to grasp the second part of the equation. The listening part.

Peter wheels himself over to the window and looks out across the lawn. It's not surprising to him that his parents are not tuned in. It's not like they ever have been. They don't care about him. Even when he was tearing up the town, shoplifting, getting drunk-and-disorderlies and citations for disrupting the peace, his cop father never said anything to him. Dad always dealt with his colleagues at the police department, somehow making most of the black marks disappear from Peter's record. But he never spoke to Peter about them. Never lectured him or asked him why he was doing what he was doing. He never even acted embarrassed that all of his friends and coworkers knew what a derelict son he had. It's like he figured if he ignored Peter's transgressions, they would go away. Maybe he thought Peter would go away. Maybe that was what he'd wanted.

Peter's mind flashes back to that birthday when he last cried in front of his mom and dad. The worst day of his life up until the day he was paralyzed. His parents have never mentioned what happened that day again. Never. Not in all these years. And his father, model police officer that he is, has never done anything to ensure that it won't happen again. Has never spoken to Peter about safety or responsibility. It's a miracle Peter has survived this long. As he stares at the glass panes of the window in front of him, he wonders for the first time how he's done it.

How has he survived for so long in a house where nothing is ever said?

• • •

Tuesday night, Jeremy watches the little family drama unfolding on his TV screen with a detachment formerly reserved only for infomercials and *Family Matters* reruns. Usually when Tara comes over on Tuesday nights to "study," they spend the first hour cuddling on the couch watching *Gilmore Girls,* which he has to this day never told any other living soul about. Then they spend the next half hour making out, then cram a few minutes of studying into the last half hour before he has to drive Tara home.

Tonight the Gilmores are on the television as usual, but Tara is just about as far away from Jeremy as a person can get while still remaining on the same piece of furniture. Jeremy looks at her profile and can tell she knows he's looking, but she doesn't take her eyes from the screen. He glances at his watch and sighs. It's been ages since her mom dropped her off, and they haven't said anything other than, "Hi . . . Do you want something to drink? . . . No thanks." Jeremy sighs again. He has no idea how to handle this situation, but he knows that not handling it at all is not going to work.

"We can watch something else," Tara says.

Jeremy picks up the remote and flicks off the TV. There's no light in the room now except the dim glow coming in through the window from the streetlamp outside. Jeremy can see half of Tara's face clearly, while the other is fuzzy in shadow.

"We have to talk about this," he says, turning sideways on the couch to face her. She does the same.

"I know it's not true," she says. She reaches out and puts her small hand over his. Jeremy feels a warm rush of love mixed with relief mixed with anxiety over lying to her. He turns his hand over and squeezes hers.

"If you know it's not true, then why are you all the way over there?" he asks.

Tara laughs and her whole face changes. The dimple comes out, her eyes scrunch up, her cheeks turn pink. She pushes a few strands of her short dark hair back behind her ear and crawls into his arms. Once he encircles her little frame in his embrace, everything else floats away, leaving only the relief. All he wants to do is kiss her. He wants to reassure her. And he wants to show himself that kissing Tara feels better than . . . than anything else.

"Don't worry about everyone," Tara says softly, resting her head on his chest just beneath his chin. She reaches up and plays with the little number-three pendant that always hangs from the chain around his neck. "Tomorrow someone will do something stupid like throw up during gym or get in a fight in the hallway, and no one will remember that story. Everything will be fine."

Jeremy tightens his arms around her. When she says it, he can almost believe it.

She tilts her head to look up at him and he puts his forehead to hers.

"I love you, Jeremy," she whispers. So sure of herself. She knows this is where she wants to be. She would never want to be anywhere else. He almost envies her.

"I love you, too," he says. Then he closes his eyes and

kisses her. A mental image of Josh appears and he instantly squelches it. He forces himself to focus on Tara. She clasps her hand around his neck, drawing him even closer, and the kissing quickly becomes more intense. Jeremy slides his hands under Tara's shirt, running his fingers along her bare back. She breaks away and looks at him, her eyelids heavy.

"Where's Emily?" she asks quietly.

"At work with my parents," Jeremy answers. "No one's here."

Tara smiles. "Just checking." She leans in and kisses him again, reaching down to pull his shirt from his jeans.

Jeremy resists the urge to tell her to stop. To turn on the lights and tell her the truth. He did kiss a guy. He *liked* kissing a guy. Let the chips fall where they may.

But he doesn't. He can't do that to her. And he can't do that to himself. Things have to stay the way they are. And he has to show Tara that she is the only one he wants. That he wants her completely.

Tara shifts her legs and turns so that she's completely facing him. When she presses into him, telling him to lie back, he doesn't resist. He leans into the pillow at the end of the couch and pulls her to him, his mouth never leaving hers.

This is right, Jeremy tells himself. *This feels right. This is perfect. This is exactly what I want. . . .*

But he can't quite make himself believe it.

CHAPTER FIVE

"I cannot believe some skeev *kissed* you, man," Mike Chumsky says, clutching the strap of his backpack as he stands in the hall by Jeremy's locker on Wednesday afternoon. "If some fag had kissed me, he'd be dead right now. Seriously. I'm talking six feet under and then some."

Jeremy tries to ignore the flash of red-hot anger that temporarily clouds his vision. He started this. He is the one who felt the need to start slurring and slamming gay guys yesterday at lunch. If he wants to dish it, he's going to have to get used to hearing it dished by slop-for-brains morons like Mike Chumsky.

"What'd he *look* like?" Mike asks, flicking his head back to get his long brown bangs off his forehead. Jeremy slams his locker so hard, it bounces right back open and needs to be slammed again.

"He looked like a guy, Chumsky," Jeremy says, moving away from his locker and into the crowded hallway. A couple of girls glance at him guiltily and Jeremy suspects they've been talking about him. They giggle the second he walks by, and he knows for sure. This type of thing has been happening all day—looks, whispers, giggles. Each time Jeremy notices somebody else noticing him, he feels a bit more conspicuous. This is getting out of hand. Everyone's talking about him. Everyone's looking. It's like he's an open target for jokes and gossip.

Everything he's worked so hard for—his normal *in*conspicuous life—is *this close* to crashing down around him. Jeremy feels like any second now he's going to walk right off the edge of his world and keep falling forever.

"Yeah, but I mean, did he *look* gay? You know, was he all, like, girly and stuff?" Mike prods. His eyes are bright with an evil-looking curiosity. Suddenly Jeremy realizes who all those morbid reality shows are pandering to. What kind of people revel in the misery and humiliation of others? He envisions himself picking Mike up by the jacket, slamming him against the wall, getting right in his face, and telling him that this is what gay looks like. Telling him to take a good look and then pounding him to a pulp.

Unfortunately, Jeremy is not Vin Diesel.

"I don't know," Jeremy says, the irritation clear in his voice. "Can we just drop it?"

Mike stops in the hallway and gapes at Jeremy like he's just suggested they quit the football team. "No, we can't just drop it," he says. "I want details. Why did the guy go after you, anyway? What was he, high or something?"

83

Jeremy feels his fists clench and open as a few people stop to look at him. People he doesn't even know standing there waiting for an answer. What the hell is he supposed to say? The truth? That Josh is pretty much the hottest guy he's ever known? Or does he say what Mike and the others want to hear? That Josh was some flighty guy with a high voice who completely fits their stereotype of what a gay guy is supposed to be?

With a start, Jeremy realizes he doesn't even know what he wants to say. In the last twenty-four hours everything has become completely confused. At least before the story came out, he knew who he was and he knew who everyone else *thought* he was. Now the lines are blurred and he doesn't even know what he's thinking anymore. All he knows is that the longer he stands there silent, the more real the panic inside him is becoming. It's like everyone in the hallway can see right through him. This feeling of being totally exposed is almost too much for Jeremy to bear.

"Hey, baby!" Tara comes rushing up to Jeremy, a delighted flush over her features. She stands on her toes and kisses him and Jeremy's little audience breaks up. The panic, unfortunately, does not. It just gets worse the moment his nostrils fill with the peachy sent of her perfume. "I haven't seen you all day!" she says, wrapping her arms around his waist.

"Yeah . . . I know," Jeremy croaks out. His mind is

suddenly filled with images from the night before. All the kissing. All the touching. All the whispers and sighs. Little beads of sweat start to form along his hairline.

"I had a great time last night," Tara says suggestively, smiling up at him.

Jeremy's stomach takes a dangerous turn, but he tries to smile. "Yeah . . . me too."

You're a liar. You're scum. You're a lying, cheating pile of spineless scum.

"I have to go," Jeremy says, pulling Tara's arms away from him and turning on his heel. Before she can stop him, he's tearing down the hall, just hoping he can get to the bathroom before he hurls.

• • •

Danny doesn't even realize he's been staring into space again until he hears the pounding of racing footsteps in the hallway and is snapped out of the atmosphere back into the confines of his own brain. He glances over at the etched glass window in the classroom door just in time to see Jeremy Mandile tear past. The bell rings and study hall officially begins. Danny looks down at the open music composition notebook in front of him. At least Jeremy is obviously losing it, too. Danny's not the only freak around here. Small consolation when his head feels like it weighs about fifty pounds.

Taking a deep breath, Danny concentrates on the tiny lines on the paper in front of him, unable to believe that the only thing he's written since he spoke with Jane yesterday is a treble clef and a couple of flat symbols. Last night, Danny spent two hours trying to write. He shifts in his seat uncomfortably just thinking about it. Truthfully, he can't call it "trying." He sat in front of the TV with his notebook open, procrastinating through bad sitcom after worse sitcom after truly awful sitcom. Every time a loud commercial blared on, he blinked, looked down at the page, and was unable, as always, to clear the fog.

Just one more show, he kept saying to himself. In fact, he'd *just-one-more-show*ed himself right to sleep.

Danny pushes his butt back in his chair until the chain attached to his wallet smacks up against the hard plastic chair back. He rolls his head from side to side, cracking his neck, then sits up straight and endeavors to clear his mind. This is study hall. There are no distractions. Well, no distractions aside from the back of Cori's head a few rows up. But he can't stare at the back of her head forever. He has to concentrate. If he can't write here, he can't write anywhere. If he can't write here, he's totally screwed.

Okay, think sax, Danny urges himself as he pulls a bit at his dark blond hair. *Great sax players. Um . . . Clarence Clemons. E Street Band. Don't think Jane would go for any Springsteen-type stuff. Okay, there's Leroi Moore. Dave Matthews Band. Interesting stuff. Some of their ballads might be good to pull from. . . .*

Okay, now he's thinking. But thinking about artists isn't going to help. He has to find a tune. Any tune. He has to get a few notes down on paper or he's definitely going to be padded-room worthy by the end of this period.

Danny tries to concentrate, tries to find music in the recesses of his mind, but before he knows it, he's staring again, this time at the blank blackboard, focusing and unfocusing his eyes and floating in the now familiar nothing.

Then he hears it. It's faint, but it's there. Eight little notes waft through the fog and dance inside Danny's ears. He'd started to slump, but he pushes himself up again, giving his head a shake and hoping it'll knock the fog out but not the notes.

His heart is pounding as he hears them again. Danny hums the notes and writes them down. His hand is shaking. It's two measures. Two tiny little measures. But it looks so beautiful written down on the page, he almost wants to cry. He did it! He got started! He hums the eight notes again and again, feeling like he'll remember them forever as the breakthrough. The moment he finally got back to—

"I love that song."

"What?" Danny blurts, earning a "shhh!" from Ms. Truder, the muumuu-wearing study hall monitor. Danny glares at Lance Haft, the innocent junior next to him. "What do you mean?"

"I mean that song you're humming," Haft whispers back, opening his hands in a gesture that clearly says,

"Duh." "Simon and Garfunkel, right? My dad used to play that album for me all the time."

Danny's stomach twists into a tight ball as he slowly looks back at the notes he's just written. His supposed salvation. He hums them in his head again. No. Not possible. He did not just write down the first line of the chorus of "Bridge Over Troubled Water," thinking it was his own. He couldn't have. He couldn't.

But he has.

Danny tears the page from his notebook and rips it and rips it and rips it until he has two handfuls of sweaty paper shards closed inside his fists. He doesn't remotely care about the stares of his classmates, half of whom have turned around to shoot him looks, some nasty, some wary, some amused.

Then his eyes fall on Cori's face. Clouded. Concerned. "Are you okay?" she mouths, a little line forming at the top of her nose.

"I'm fine," Danny mouths back, mortified that Cori was here to witness his minor breakdown.

I'm just a freak, Danny thinks as Cori turns in her seat again, apparently believing him. He clenches his teeth as he lets the paper shower to the floor at his sides. He can't stay on this medication anymore. He can't. Not if it makes him this brain-dead. Not if it makes him this . . . stupid. *I hate this, I hate this, I hate this, I hate this. . . .*

But the anger quickly fades and then he's staring again,

any emotion caught up in the fog and floating slowly away, leaving the old numbness in its place.

• • •

"Can I help you?"

Meena looks up from the birthday card she's staring at to find the chubby man who used to be sitting behind the counter standing right next to her. His bright yellow sweater is too much color against the muted light in the Hallmark store. It's gotten so dark and gray outside, it's put a dreary dullness over everything, matching Meena's mood.

"No thanks," Meena says, forcing a smile so he won't think she's the street urchin she's sure she looks like.

"Well, let me know if you need anything," he says. His eyes are wary as he walks away—an expression Meena's gotten used to seeing. People used to smile when they saw her. They used to stare because she was pretty. Now they're afraid of her. Meena's heart turns painfully as she realizes this, and suddenly she needs to get out of here. She shoves the card back into the little slot, zips her jacket up to her chin, and heads outside.

The blast of wind and rain that hits her face knocks the air out of her lungs. Meena uses her palms to push her stringy hair off her face and lifts her hood. It doesn't do much good. She's already soaked. She blinks a few times in a vain attempt to clear the rain from her lashes and lids and looks around, desperate for a place she can stay inside for more than fifteen minutes. Her body aches to go home to her bed, but she can't. And the fact that she can't makes her heart hurt with an intensity she's never felt before.

Home was all she had left. Her only safe place. And now he's taken that from her, too. Steven has taken everything.

The tears overflow, mixing with the rain as she shivers in front of the glowing pink Hallmark sign in the window. She has no place to go. No place. Why is this happening to her?

Meena hears a car door slam and looks across the rain-battered street to see Jeremy Mandile running up the steps to the halfway house. Weird. What would Mr. All-American Jock be doing at *that* place? But then she vaguely remembers that Jeremy's parents are some sort of philanthropists or something and are involved with the house. She sniffles and stares at the warm yellow light emanating through the front windows. The whole place exudes warmth, even through the wet bitterness outside. Before Meena can really think it through, she's crossing the street and walking in the front door.

It does not disappoint. The moment she takes off her jacket, she feels like she's being enveloped in warmth. Jeremy is standing at the front desk and turns when he hears the door close. He can't hide his surprise when he sees Meena standing there, looking, she's sure, like a dirty, semidrowned rat.

Still, Meena feels a bit better just seeing Jeremy there. Even though they hung out in the same crowd until recently, she and Jeremy have never been close. But she knows Jeremy is a good person. And she hopes he won't ask too many questions.

"Hey," Jeremy says, remembering himself and wiping the surprise away. "What are you doing here?"

Question number one. Meena has no idea what she's doing here, so she just shrugs.

Jeremy moves a few steps closer. For a split second, she's afraid he's going to touch her and she flinches ever so slightly. Concern registers in his eyes, but at least Jeremy's concern looks real—unlike that of all the guidance counselors, coaches, and teachers who have tried to talk to her in the past week or so.

"Are you okay?" Jeremy asks.

Meena almost bursts into tears but is saved when Mrs. Mandile breezes into the room.

"Mom!" Jeremy says, leaning over to give her a peck on the cheek. "This is my friend Meena Miller," he says. Meena smiles. She can't believe he called her his friend. She hasn't even spoken to him in weeks. But then, he'd probably call anyone from school his friend. Jeremy's that kind of guy—generous, sweet, loved by all. He's probably never had a real problem in his life. Except . . . well, but that was a long time ago.

"Hello!" Mrs. Mandile says with a welcoming smile. "I remember you from when you were just this big," she says, holding out her hand by her waist. "It's so nice to see you,

Meena. I hope you'll stay for dinner. We're serving Jeremy's favorite."

Meena is a mess of unshed tears, relief, surprise, unworthiness, and gratefulness. She couldn't have found her voice if she tried.

"It's this amazing beef stew," Jeremy explains, his eyes actually lighting up. "And we get this huge crusty bread from Back Street Bakery." He smiles at her and there's no pity there, just kindness. "If you stay, I'll get you extra butter."

"Thanks," Meena says. She feels herself smile. "I'll stay."

• • •

Jeremy's heart is pounding as he shows Meena into the large room that serves as a dining area for the halfway house. While he's grateful that Meena hasn't said anything about the rumors at school, his insides are also freaking out since he knows that Josh is probably around somewhere. He has no idea how he's going to act if he sees Josh, and now that someone from school is here, he's going to have to watch his every move even more closely.

The moment they walk into the room, Jeremy scans the tables and folding chairs, trying to find a place for himself and Meena to sit and trying not to make it too obvious that he's looking for Josh. There are about twenty or so men and women gathered in various groups around the warm room, eating and talking. Jeremy has always liked the cozy feeling of the dining area. His mother decorated it kind of like a ski lodge, with wood-paneled walls, heavy green drapes, and wildlife paintings. There are almost never any fights or outbursts in this room. It's probably that fact that has made it Jeremy's favorite since he was a kid.

Finally, when he can avoid it no longer, Jeremy checks the opposite wall to see who's working behind the serving counter. He immediately spots Josh dishing up stew from one of the huge metal warming pots. Jeremy's heart skips a few beats, then continues its pounding. Every bone in his body tells him to flee, but he can't. He has to deal with this sometime. He realizes he's frozen in one spot and glances at Meena to see if she's noticed his bizarre behavior, but she seems to have taken a serious interest in biting her cuticles.

Something is definitely wrong here. In her baggy clothes and muddy sneakers and with her stringy hair clearly unwashed, Meena doesn't even look like Meena anymore. He resolves to get the Josh thing over with, then come back here and see if he can help. Maybe Meena needs some real help, and if there's one thing Jeremy has always been good at, it's listening. Buoyed by the idea of having something to focus on other than his own problems, Jeremy pulls out a chair for Meena.

"Hey, why don't you sit here and I'll go get us some food?" he says.

Meena plops into the chair and continues to gnaw on the side of one of her fingers. She rolls her eyes up to glance at Jeremy. "Thanks."

Suddenly Jeremy's throat tightens. The way Meena looks

at him causes his mind to form an image of the last time he saw that expression on her face, the last time she looked as miserable and . . . *scared* as she does now. Back when they were real friends and they used to play together all the time. But the image he's seeing isn't from a happy play date. It's an image from the day Jeremy's life changed forever.

"I just want to go home," Meena had said to him that day. *"Can't I just go home?"*

Simply thinking about it makes Jeremy's heart break all over again.

Then someone brushes by him and Jeremy snaps out of it. Snaps back into the present.

"Uh . . . no problem," he says. He wipes his sweaty palms against his thighs a few times, then once against the backs of his legs for good measure. As he crosses the room slowly, stopping occasionally to let a tenant get by with his or her food, Jeremy keeps his eyes on Josh, waiting for him to look up. Is he going to see him and look quickly away? Is he going to see him and smile? Is he going to see him and feel as totally and completely awkward as Jeremy does?

Jeremy gets all the way to the serving table before Josh notices him. He holds his breath for the moment of truth. Josh takes one look at him, turns his head, and sneezes. Big.

"Bless you," Jeremy says, somehow keeping the elation out of his voice. Josh wasn't avoiding him—he really was sick! *Is* sick, from the looks of it. Red nose. Pale face. Watery eyes. Josh looks like crap! This is great!

"Thanks," Josh says. He grabs a tissue from a box on a chair behind him and wipes his nose, then smiles apologetically. "It's . . . good to see you," he says, crumpling the tissue and stuffing it in the front pocket of his cords. Then, more quietly: "Sorry I haven't called. I've just been really sick and I wasn't sure . . ." He trails off and flushes, glancing around to see if anyone's paying attention. They're not. The other workers are busy serving food, and the tenants probably couldn't care less what two teenage boys are talking about.

Jeremy looks down at the table, trying to control his own blush. His heart is fluttering like crazy. He's never felt anything like this before and he's surprised at the intensity. All this time he thought Josh was avoiding him, and apparently he was waiting to see how Jeremy felt. He presses his fingertips into the checkered tablecloth and takes a deep breath. He hadn't been sure how he'd feel at this moment, but it's definitely relief that's flowing through him. Relief and excitement.

"Yeah . . . no . . . that's okay," Jeremy says, cringing at his inarticulateness. Now it's Josh's turn to look down at the table. This can't go on. Pretty soon this conversation is going to start to look conspicuous.

"So, do you really think that serving food is the best place for you to be right now?" Jeremy jokes as Josh sniffles loudly.

Cracking a smile, Josh shrugs. "Yeah, you're probably

right," he says. "I'll ask your mom to take over and go file or something."

"Sounds like a plan," Jeremy says, happy that the awkward moment has passed. He feels like he should say something more, but he has no idea what it is. Josh gathers his things—backpack, tissue box, bottle of water—then turns back to Jeremy.

"Will I see you later?" he asks, looking Jeremy directly in the eye.

He still wants to talk, too, Jeremy realizes, his heart somehow skipping even faster.

"Yeah . . . definitely," Jeremy says. They both smile small smiles and then Josh disappears into the kitchen to find Jeremy's mother.

Jeremy doesn't start breathing again until Josh is gone. He picks up a couple of bowls and dishes up some stew for himself and Meena, trying to look normal. Trying not to look like he just shared a moment with another guy. But inside, he feels like he's falling apart. He knows he promised himself to tell Josh he wasn't interested. He promised himself that he would just get on with his life. But how can he?

How can he ignore something that makes him feel like this?

CHAPTER SiX

"**I can't believe** you're actually buying it!" Gemma exclaims, leaning into the Banana Republic counter and snapping her gum as Karyn hands her mother's credit card over to the slick-looking guy behind the register. He smiles a knowing smile at her. Like he gets what it feels like when you just *have* to have something. Karyn smiles back, even though that's not what she's feeling. She saw the jacket, she thought it would look cool with her favorite brown jeans, and she felt like buying something. End of story. So what if it was a two-hundred-dollar purchase? She'll deal with her mom later. Or not. There's always the chance dear old mom will never even notice the charge.

Karyn signs her mother's name on the receipt and Slick Boy hands her back the credit card without even glancing at the signature. Not so slick after all. She and Gemma join Jeannie, Amy, and Cara Zellick, who are sitting on a bench across from Sam Goody, opening the plastic wrappers on their new CDs.

"What did you get?" Cara asks in a half gasp as her eyes widen at the size of Karyn's bag. Cara is always excited about everything. Sometimes it gets on Karyn's nerves, but tonight she's not letting anything bother her. Technically she's breaking her grounding, so she figures she might as well live it up.

"Just a jacket," Karyn says with a shrug.

"Right. Just the most luscious leather jacket ever," Gemma adds.

Cara whimpers. "Lemme see!"

"Can we *please* take it down a notch?" Jeannie says, rolling her eyes.

Karyn is saved from the chore of showing off the jacket by the appearance of Reed, Shaheem Dobi, Mike Chumsky, and Carlos Ruiz, walking through the mall side by side in a perfect unbroken line of blue-and-gold jackets. They look like they're auditioning to be extras in Kevin Williamson's next bad teen movie. Still, she's always happy to see Reed.

"Hey, baby!" Gemma calls out, running like a little girl over to Carlos and planting her lips on his. He lifts her up and Karyn wouldn't be surprised to see Gemma wrap her legs around the kid right there in the mall. Apparently she's officially over the whole salty chicken humiliation.

"God! Get a room!" Jeannie says with a groan. She's definitely in a mood. Must've missed that fifth cup of coffee.

As the guys and girls meld into a little crowd, Karyn finds herself drifting to the side. Even though she's trying to be Chipper Girl, she's not in the mood to watch her friends flirt and squeal and bat their eyelashes. She smiles when she sees that Reed is drifting with her. They shuffle off silently until they're out of earshot of their raucous friends and lean against one of the mall's many huge, prehistoric-looking potted plants.

"So, how's everything?" Reed asks, his blue eyes shadowed by the omnipresent baseball cap.

"Good," she says. It's more of a squawk than a word.

"Still haven't talked to your mom, huh?" he asks.

"Nope," Karyn says. At school that day she'd told Reed about the icy veil of silence that has fallen over her house since Monday night. Her mother, shockingly enough, hasn't been around much. But when she is, the deathly quiet is practically tangible.

"Well, this has happened with you guys before," Reed says, looking over at their friends. Carlos lifts his hands above his head comically, clearly telling a story, and the rest of the crowd laughs. Karyn can't help thinking that the scene looks like something out of a soda commercial. "By tomorrow night you'll be sitting at the kitchen table with her, eating Ben & Jerry's right out of the carton, and all will be right in the world of Aufiero."

Karyn cracks a smile even though her heart pangs with a bit of longing for the picture he paints. Reed is right, and it makes her feel a little bit better. She and her mother have had monster arguments before and the stalemate has almost always been broken by the sharing of junk food. One joins the other at the table and eventually they're chatting about the latest marketing ploy by the makeup companies, and all is forgotten.

"Thanks," Karyn says, leaning her head on his solid shoulder. "You always know what to say."

Reed takes in a breath. "That's what I'm here for."

This sentiment makes Karyn's smile grow even wider.

Then he clears his throat. "Have you spoken to T. J. lately?"

Karyn picks up her head and Reed shifts his weight, ending up just a touch farther away from Karyn than he was a moment before. "Last night," she says. "You?"

"Called him just before I came here," Reed says. Pulling his cell phone out of his pocket, he presses a few buttons and frowns down at the little screen, then replaces it. "He was on his way out for pizza with some people on his floor. Said he'd call me back."

Karyn swallows. "People?" she says. "Like guys and girls? Girl-type people?"

Reed turns to look at her, his eyes shining with a smile, his mouth dropped open in pretend shock. "Is Karyn Aufiero actually insecure about other girls?"

"Of course not!" Karyn says, shoving him with her shoulder. She scoffs, even though her insides are twisted up as she pictures the Denise Richards girl again, this time lowering herself into T. J.'s lap at some seedy pizza joint. She really has to have her imagination surgically removed.

Suddenly Karyn's friends descend on her and Reed in a whirl of perfume and hair spray.

"We're going to the drugstore!" Cara announces as Amy pulls Karyn away from Reed.

"I guess I'll see you later!" Karyn says over her shoulder, allowing herself to be dragged off by her friends. Reed lifts his hand and before Karyn knows it, she's standing in an aisle under a blinking fluorescent light, staring at a slew of colorfully packaged condoms.

"Um, what are we doing here?" she asks, glancing at her friends.

"Cara has to get ready for her date with Dean Turkowski this weekend," Gemma explains, picking up a blue box and thrusting it at Cara. "These are the best ones."

"Why does *Cara* have to be prepared?" Karyn asks. She grabs a pink box and turns it over, raising her eyebrows at the silhouettes of two naked bodies on the back. "Shouldn't Dean be the one with the stash?"

"Please," Jeannie says, checking her lipstick in her compact. "These guys can't even remember to put on a little deodorant."

Karyn is suddenly struck with a vision of the Denise Richards girl walking, no *strutting*, into T. J.'s room with a box of condoms. Before she can stop her brain from taking it any further, T. J. and Denise are fully naked, climbing into his bed under the blue-and-green-plaid sheets that Karyn bought him at Bed Bath & Beyond before he left for school.

"So, these are the best?" she asks, grabbing a blue box from the shelf.

She ignores her friends' squeals of joy as she heads up to the front counter. This isn't an occasion for squealing. This is a huge, huge deal. This is a huge deal because it means she's deciding that it's possible. It's a huge deal because for the first time, she's not freezing up at the thought of sex.

As she places the box down next to the register, she sees herself in T. J.'s arms. Sees the way he looks at her each time he sees her—like he's looking at a princess or a beauty queen. Like he's so lucky just to be with her. And she knows, at that moment at least, that taking this step is right. She's not deciding that she's definitely going to do it, but she is taking a step closer.

And because she knows that, she's not hearing Jeannie say she's proud of her. She's not hearing Gemma tell her she won't regret it or Amy telling her not to expect too much the first time. She pays no attention to the fact that Cara's practically hyperventilating at the thought of Karyn having sex with T. J.—the guy who last year was named not only best looking, but best athlete and most school-spirited. All she's hearing is her own mind reeling.

"So, you decided to go through with it?" Amy whispers to Karyn as she shakily hands over a ten-dollar bill. Karyn just smiles. She hasn't decided that. Not quite yet. But she feels like she's come one step closer to eradicating Denise Richards from her head.

• • •

Wednesday evening, Danny sits on the thin carpet in his bedroom, cross-legged, holding his head in his hands. His fingers tug at his hair. He is more than aware that if anyone were to walk in, they'd think he was in the midst of a nervous breakdown, but he doesn't care. Let them. Maybe if they see him like this, they'll realize how bad things have gotten and let him deal. Let him go off his meds. Let him feel like a person again.

It's getting worse. Worse every day. Every time he takes those little pills, he loses a little more. A little more of his mind. A little more of his consciousness.

Strewn on the floor around Danny are dozens of CDs, each containing a song that Danny has "written" this afternoon. Ever since the Simon and Garfunkel debacle in study hall that day, Danny has been hearing strains of music, thinking they're his own creations, and then realizing they've been around for ten, twenty, thirty years. Each time this happens, Danny pops the offending CD into his disc player and listens to the song, as if to prove to himself that he actually is that stupid.

Now Danny stares down at the carnival-clown-type monster on the cover of his Lifehouse CD, focusing on the wicked eyes that laugh back at him.

You'll never be anything, a little voice in Danny's head tells him. *You'll never be anything if you stay like this. What kind of life is this with no feeling? What's the point, Danny? What's the point?*

Danny crosses his arms over his chest and grips himself, rocking forward and back. Why does he have to be like this? All he wants is to be normal. All of his friends are normal. Why did he have to be born with this *problem* in his brain? Why did he have to be born a freak? It's not fair. He just wants to be normal. Everything would be fine if he could just be normal. He'd be good. He'd be happy. He'd be normal.

Cry, dammit. Danny knows he wants to cry, but he can't. He can't even get his eyes to water. *Freak. Freak. Freak. Freak. Freak.*

Danny lets out a loud, wordless shout, reaches up and grabs his huge CD towers with both hands, and shoves them over. CDs clatter and crash and crack. Jewel cases fly in all directions. One of the towers splits in the middle and lies broken on the floor. The noise is huge. The noise should be satisfying. It's not.

Footsteps pound on the stairs and Danny pushes

himself to his feet, hurdles the mess, and flies toward his bedroom door. He flips the lock just before the doorknob starts to turn.

"Danny! What *was* that? Are you all right? What did you do?"

Danny doesn't answer. His mother pleads with him to answer her, but he won't. He can't take this anymore. If she won't listen to him, what's the point of talking to her? Danny walks over to his bed and drops down on top of the covers. He lies on his side, curls up in a ball, and pulls his comforter over his head, making a little tent. A little pocket of softness.

His mother is still talking, but Danny blocks it out. All he wants to do is feel. Something. Anything. That's all he wants. Maybe there's a way. Maybe he can find a—

But before Danny can even finish his thought, he's drifting off to sleep.

• • •

Wednesday evening, after their shift at the halfway house, Jeremy sits with Josh at the diner, nursing a cup of coffee and jumping every time the door opens.

"Expecting someone?" Josh asks, leaning back in the brown vinyl seat as Jeremy glances over his shoulder at the entrance for about the thirtieth time.

"No," Jeremy answers, embarrassed. They both know why he keeps looking. This place is kind of a Falls High hangout, and even though Josh doesn't know what's been going on with Jeremy at school, he has to know Jeremy doesn't want anyone to see them together and get the sense that they're, well, *together*. Considering he's met Jeremy's girlfriend, he'd have to be an idiot not to figure that one out.

Jeremy didn't really want to come here, but the diner is the closest eatery to the halfway house and Jeremy was so nervous when he and Josh left work, he hadn't been able to even think of anywhere else to go.

"So, who was the girl you came in with tonight?" Josh asks. His arm is lying across the top of his seat and he's picking at the corner seam of the booth. Jeremy wonders if he's jealous. What does Josh think, that not only did he cheat on Tara with him, but that he has another girl on the side as well?

"She's a friend from school," Jeremy says, shifting in his seat as he recalls the nonconversation he had with Meena over dinner. She'd answered every single question he asked with a "yes" or a "no" even if they weren't yes-or-no questions. He'd given up after about ten minutes and they'd just eaten in silence. "I think something's going on at home, maybe. She used to be this pretty, popular, friendly person, but lately she's been a total mess. She bailed the second we were done eating and wouldn't take a ride home no matter how many times I offered."

"Well, you know there's only so much you can do,"

Josh says earnestly. He leans forward slightly, warming both hands on the sides of his coffee mug. *At least he seems better than he did earlier,* Jeremy thinks. Josh had swigged some medicine before they left the halfway house. Jeremy can't help noticing that Josh somehow seems older than he is. He has a self-assured presence that only the adults in Jeremy's life seem to have. "You can't help someone unless they want to be helped."

Jeremy snorts a laugh. "You sound like my dad," he says.

"I think that's where I got that line," Josh shoots back with a smile.

Jeremy's heart squeezes and he takes a deep breath. This is serious. Every single time Josh smiles, Jeremy's heart reacts in some way or another. He's never had palpitations over anyone before—not even Tara.

An awkward silence falls over the table and Jeremy knows they both want to bring up what happened the other night, but every time he tries to say the words, they get stuck somewhere between his throat and his tongue. He has to say *something*. If not, they're going to sit here all night in this void, and he's pretty sure he'll lose it if—

Josh sighs. "So—"

"I don't know what I'm doing here," Jeremy blurts out. He flushes so hard and fast, he's sure his skin is going to burn right off.

He could leave. Get up and walk out right now. Go back to Tara and his life and forget Josh ever existed. But for some reason, he can't make his legs move.

Josh leans forward, forearms on the table, voice just above a whisper. "It's okay, Jeremy."

Jeremy takes one look at Josh's open, honest face and feels something inside of him shift. If there was ever a time to spill, this is it. If there was ever a person he could trust on this subject, Josh is the one. Jeremy takes a deep breath. After all these years of bottling a significant part of himself up, talking is not easy.

"Someone from school saw us . . . at the party," Jeremy begins, keeping his voice down. He waits for a reaction, and when Josh's brown eyes register sympathy and not dread, Jeremy rushes on. "The last couple of days have been torture. Everyone has been talking and laughing behind my back. And I . . . uh . . . I denied everything." He swallows and glances at Josh, expecting him to scoff at him or tell him he's a fake or a fraud or a liar. But Josh's expression doesn't change. He wants Jeremy to go on. Jeremy pushes his hands through his hair at the temples and forces himself to sit up straight. "I just don't know if I'm ready for this, you know?" he says. "I know you think I'm a wuss, but—"

"I understand," Josh says matter-of-factly. "Just because I'm out doesn't mean I don't remember what it's like."

Jeremy can't keep the relief from washing over his face.

Josh laughs. "God! What did you think I was going to do? Renounce you as a bad gay person or something?" He takes a sip of his coffee and leans back in his seat again, smiling.

Shaking his head, Jeremy tries to laugh as well, but it comes out a little forced. *A gay person.* It's the first time Jeremy's been identified that way out loud. He doesn't even know what to feel about that—the label feels awkward, wrong. Yet somehow it also feels more true than anything he's heard about himself in a long time. And *that's* downright terrifying.

"I don't know what I thought," Jeremy says after his weak laughter dies away. He gulps at his tepid decaf, replaces the cup in its saucer, and then rubs his face with his hands. "I don't know what the hell I'm doing."

Josh is staring down at his cup of coffee and Jeremy can tell from his face that he's contemplating something. Jeremy's stomach turns with nervousness.

"What?" he asks, not sure he wants to know the answer. "What are you thinking?"

"I'm just wondering what your relationship is like with your girlfriend," Josh says, glancing up for a split second and then refocusing on his coffee as if it's too difficult to hold Jeremy's gaze.

At that moment Jeremy feels the guilty rush of what he's doing crash over him like a crippling wave. Tara. What would Tara do if she knew who Jeremy was with right now and what they were talking about? If she knew how Jeremy was feeling about this amazing, patient, perfect guy sitting across the table from him? If she knew how many times in the last hour he'd recalled the kiss he and Josh had shared on Friday night? He tries to push Tara out of his mind, but he can't. Her face is there now, in his mind, glaring at him. And she's not going anywhere.

Jeremy opens his mouth to answer Josh's question, but as he studies Josh's face, he knows Josh doesn't actually want an answer. On the surface he's the picture of indifferent curiosity, but beneath it there's obvious hope and fear. In a rush Jeremy realizes that Josh really likes him. As much as Jeremy likes Josh. It's not just Tara's feelings that are riding on Jeremy; it's Josh's as well.

The pulling sensation Jeremy felt in the hallway at school that afternoon starts up again, but this time it's fifty times more intense. There's a pull toward Tara and his life as he knows it. A pull toward Josh and maintaining this pleasant, queasy, crushy feeling he's had all night. And there's a pull to disappear. For a moment that's the strongest of all because it seems to be the only scenario in which no one will get hurt. Once again Jeremy almost gets up and walks away from the table, never to look back, but he can't imagine what his next move would be after that, so he just stays rooted to the spot. Mute.

Then the door opens, and even in his schizoid state Jeremy turns around. It's Meena. And she's soaked through. She pulls off her jacket, darkened with rain, and snaps it once, sending droplets flying across the room.

"Hey, Meena!" Jeremy says. He's partially concerned and partially relieved to have someone else to focus on. To get out of his head and heart for a moment.

She glances up quickly and her eyes look almost frantic.

"It's just me," Jeremy says, lifting his hand.

She looks around her. Looks at the door. Seems to think better of bolting out into the rain. Jeremy's concern mounts. Why would she want to run from him?

"Hey," she says finally, approaching the table. She watches Josh like she's sure he's going to spring out of the chair and attack her. Like a stranger is somehow threatening. For the first time, Jeremy starts to wonder if she's on something.

"Are you okay?" he asks. "I thought you were going home."

Meena shrugs one shoulder. "Yeah . . . me too."

Jeremy glances at Josh, whose look reflects his own. *What's going on with this girl?*

"Hi, sweetie!" The large waitress who has been serving Josh and Jeremy walks up behind Meena and pats her shoulder like they're old friends. "How's that arm doing?"

Jeremy's eyes instinctively go to Meena's forearm, where

111

he sees a small, circular burn before she can slap her hand over it. It looks like somebody put out a cigarette in her flesh. Jeremy glances up at Meena, eyes wide, and immediately realizes it was a mistake. She takes one look at his face and tears out the door. She doesn't even put her jacket back on.

"Excuse me," Jeremy says to Josh. Josh just nods his understanding as Jeremy gets up and runs after Meena. He doesn't know what he's going to say to her or what he's going to do, but he has to find out if she's okay.

Outside, Jeremy stands under the awning and looks around the parking lot, but Meena is already gone. Gone or hiding. He calls her name a couple of times but gets no response. Jeremy crosses his arms over his chest, pulling his jacket closer to him as he shivers. This has been one hell of a weird day. Avoiding Tara, almost pummeling Mike, barfing in the bathroom for the first time in over three years of high school. Seeing Meena at the halfway house, facing Josh and this obviously huge crush, and now seeing Meena all freaked out again. He almost can't believe this has all happened in one day.

He glances up at the window where Josh is sitting, not ready to go inside yet. Taking a deep breath, Jeremy looks up at the rainy sky and lets it out slowly, watching the steam disappear into the air. For the first time, he knows with an absolute certainty that he has to do something about this Josh thing. He can't ignore feelings this strong.

Sooner or later something will happen and someone is going to get hurt—most likely Tara. And he can't bear the thought of hurting her. He does love her. She's his best friend in the whole world.

And she deserves to know the truth.

• • •

Meena is surrounded by laughter. It's the carefree, unadulterated, loud, gasping laughter of eight children. It fills Meena's whole body with a light and airy glee. She looks around and finds she's sitting on the floor in a familiar yet strange room. There's a big couch with frays and tears all over the bottom as if a hundred cats had earned their claws there. Suddenly Jane Scott crosses the room and takes Meena's hand, pulling her up off the throw rug she'd been sitting on.

"Where're we going?" Meena asks. Her voice sounds eerily young.

"Come on! Let's play!" Jane says, her smile exposing tiny, pearly teeth and one big gap at the front.

Meena skips after her friend happily, but when she sees they're heading for a closet, a cold shot of fear streaks down her spine. Meena digs in her feet. She doesn't want to go over there. She's petrified, but she can't seem to speak.

I don't want to, *she thinks.* Let me go! I don't want to go there!

But Jane keeps pulling and pulling her, inching her forward.

"Come on, Meena!" Jane says, looking back, still laughing.

She has no idea what she's about to do and Meena can't find the voice to tell her. "Come on! It'll be fun!"

No, it won't! *Meena's mind screams as she struggles against Jane's impossibly strong grip. Don't do it, Jane! Don't open the door! I'm scared! I'm scared!*

She watches as Jane's little hand reaches forward toward the little glass handle on the closet door. Meena suddenly feels like she's seen this closet before. She could have told Jane exactly where the white paint was chipped and that the handle would stick a bit before Jane finally got it to turn.

No, Jane! Don't!

"NO!" Meena finally shouts aloud, but it's as if Jane can't hear her. She reaches out and opens the door and Meena screams in horror.

Steven Clayton is standing there. And he's smiling right at her.

"No!" Meena gasps, sitting straight up in bed. Before she's even fully awake, her eyes dart to her bedroom door and her blood runs cold. The sliver of golden light under her door is broken by two dark, round shadows. Shadows the size of feet.

A petrified tear spills over onto Meena's cheek as the doorknob turns.

It's locked. It's locked. It's locked, she tells herself as the doorknob clicks. But that doesn't stop him. He tries it again. Absurdly, Meena is suddenly sure that Steven is going to find a way into her room. The lock will only deter him for so long. Her eyes dart frantically across her room to the armchair in the far corner. In one noiseless motion Meena swings to the floor and flies across the room. Her feet barely touch the carpet, but she feels like she's making the noise of a family of elephants.

She grabs the arms of the chair and pulls at it, bending at the waist to give it all her strength. It moves slowly, thanks to the carpeting her dad had installed in her room last spring. The doorknob keeps turning and clicking, turning and clicking. Meena envisions Steven standing out there with a bobby pin, going at the lock like a world-class thief.

Finally she gets the chair in front of the door and pushes it right up against it, lodging the back of the chair under the doorknob as she's seen done in so many movies. She takes one step back, her arms at her sides, staring at the doorknob.

"Meena."

He says her name in a whisper and she almost chokes.

"Meena, honey, it's me. . . . I can hear you."

Meena covers her mouth with her hand as tears squeeze silently from her eyes and pour down her face. She lowers herself unsteadily onto the edge of her bed, bracing her free hand on the mattress at her side.

Go away. Please go away, she begs silently. She wishes

her father would come out and find him—make him explain. She wishes her brothers were home. The guys
barely slept, and Steven would never have dared come
out here.

"Meena," he tries one last time. His whisper is harsher—
almost desperate.

Meena tries to breathe. She doesn't move a muscle. She
just watches the sliver under the door until finally, finally he
walks away. Then she curls up on top of her covers and sobs.

CHAPTER SEVEN

Jeremy tries to concentrate on the road as he drives Tara toward Phil's for lunch on Thursday, but he stops a little bit too late at every light and takes every corner a little too quickly. His mind is not on driving.

You can do this. You have to do this. Telling Tara will make the guilt go away. And you can't live with the guilt. He glances at her from the corner of his eye and sees that she's gripping the little handle above her window like she's holding on for dear life.

"You okay?" Jeremy asks. He knows she's not. And she's about to be *very* not okay. But it feels like the right thing to ask at the time.

"Uh . . . yeah," Tara says, flicking her short brown hair away from her face and loosening her grip just slightly. He notices how her dark red sweater brightens her whole face. She looks beautiful. Then he realizes how entirely inappropriate the thought is at this moment and turns his gaze back to the road. His mind is sick. "Are *you* okay?" Tara asks.

"Yeah! Why?" Jeremy blurts out. A horn honks behind him and he glances up to find that the light has turned green. He slams on the gas and he and Tara are both pressed back into their seats. When he takes his foot off the pedal in reaction, they pitch forward slightly. Jeremy wipes his palm across his forehead, but they're both equally wet with sweat.

"Sure. You're *fine*," Tara says, rolling her eyes and smiling. The smile is like a butcher knife to Jeremy's heart. She doesn't know what's about to happen. She's completely oblivious. "That's why you're driving like my little brother in his Power Wheels."

This isn't right, Jeremy thinks. *You've already waited too long. You've already done enough to her. Fooling around with her on Tuesday night? What kind of bastard move was that? You have to tell her. You have to tell her. You have to—*

"Jeremy, don't take this the wrong way, but you're sweating like a pig," Tara says, all concern. "What is going on?"

All right. That's it.

Jeremy pulls into the first parking lot he sees—the deserted lot around a lighting shop that's been closed for months. He kills the engine and stares through the windshield at the brown weeds that line the asphalt. How does a person begin a conversation like this?

"Why are we stopping here?" Tara asks. There's a pause. "Jeremy, you're starting to scare me here. What's going on?"

Jeremy wants to look at her. He knows that he should. But he can't bring himself to do it. He's never felt like this in his life—like the scum of the earth. He would give almost anything to not have to do this to Tara. To not make her see him this way.

"There's something I have to tell you," Jeremy begins. He thinks about stopping right there. That was hard enough to say and he hasn't said anything yet. But he makes himself continue. "It's about me. And it's not good."

Great. Very articulate.

Tara lets out a nervous laugh. "What could you possibly say about yourself that would be *that* not good?"

He attempts a glance in her direction, but she looks scared now. Tight. Like every cell in her body is on the defensive. She knows him well enough to know that something is very wrong. Jeremy swallows back the bile that's rising in his throat and brings his hands to grip the top of the steering wheel.

"I want you to know that this isn't about you," he says. There are tears in his eyes. Tears in his voice. His heart is pounding in a sickening, heavy way and he's sure that if and when he finally gets this out, he's going to vomit.

"Omigod. Are you breaking up with me?" Tara blurts out. There are tears in her voice, too. "Jeremy. Look at me." He does. And he knows she can read the guilt, the fear, and the truth in his eyes. Somehow she pulls back farther toward the door. Her petite body looks even smaller.

119

"Wait a minute. You're not . . . It's not . . ." She turns away for a moment and swallows hard. She blinks a few times. When she looks back again, her sweet, beautiful face is as hard as stone. "It's not true, is it? Are you . . . gay? Did you really kiss that guy?"

Jeremy says nothing. He couldn't if he tried. But that's enough.

"Omigod. Omigod." She bends forward in her seat, her short, smooth hair almost covering her face as she hyperventilates. "No. It's not true. This can't be happening," she says, bringing her hand to her chest.

"Tara." Jeremy reaches out his hand to touch her back. All he wants to do is comfort her and be there for her like he has through everything from her mother's hospital stay last year to her embarrassing student government loss this past September. But before he can touch her, her left arm flies up and whacks his hand away. Hard.

Jeremy's heart plummets as Tara sits up and glares at him. He's never seen her look at him like this before. He's never seen her look at *anyone* like this before. Her skin is so, so pale but covered with very red blotches.

"How could you do this to me?" she squeaks out, tears spilling down her cheeks. "I thought you loved me. I thought we were in love. And . . . oh God! What about Tuesday night?"

She says the last few words in total disgust. Jeremy can't move. He can't breathe. She hates him. She's revolted by him.

This is worse than he'd ever imagined. And he'd imagined horrors. She pulls up her legs and hugs them to her, squeezing herself as far away from Jeremy as she can possibly get.

"I want to go back," she says clearly. Evenly.

Jeremy can't handle this. He has to try to make her understand. "Tara, I was hoping we could talk about this. I—"

"Take me back to school," she says. Her eyes are flat as she stares out at the bright blue sky. "I never want to talk to you again."

● ● ●

Keep it going. . . . Come on, Karyn. . . . You're almost there.

Karyn pushes herself as hard as she can, even though her upper legs are quivering like Jell-O. Her sweat is drying on her skin in the cold midafternoon air, but all she can think about is how good this run feels. She hasn't thought about her mother or T. J. once in the last ten minutes and . . . oops, she just thought about them both. She sees a bunch of the guys standing by the finish line, gaping at her as if they've never seen a girl run before, and she runs even harder.

"Nine minutes, fifty-four seconds!" Ms. Sutton calls out as Karyn's feet pound into the dirt just past the cross-country course's makeshift finish line. "Nice run, Aufiero."

Karyn manages to get out a "thanks" as she walks it off, sucking in air. She knows her face is beet red, her hair is sticking in strings to her neck, and her eyes are watering from the cold, but she tries not to think about it. She just wants to hang on to the adrenaline high as long as possible.

"Okay, Karyn, what's going on?"

Karyn resists the urge to spit out her extra saliva, takes another deep breath, and looks up at Reed. His hair is plastered to his head and his skin is the bright pink color of a fresh sunburn. Just looking at him and knowing she's not the only one in desperate need of a shower makes her feel a little better. But not enough.

"What do you mean?" she asks, placing her hands on her hips and starting across the football field toward the school. "Nothing's going on."

"Yeah, right. You just participated in gym class for the first time since we won the square-dancing contest in fourth grade," Reed says. "Something tells me you guys haven't called a junk food truce at your house yet."

Karyn sighs and pulls off her sweatshirt as she walks, exposing the well-worn T-shirt beneath. The blast of cold air against her bare arms feels as good as a cool shower. "Nope. No truces. Things basically suck, if you want to know the truth." She raises her shoulders and rolls them back, trying to get rid of the knots that seem to have permanently taken up residence there. "I am way too young to need a chiropractor," she says, moving her head from side to side.

Without a pause Reed steps behind her and puts his hands on her shoulders, kneading his thumbs into her back as she walks. Karyn almost moans in relief as the muscles start to loosen but stops herself in time. There are people walking and talking around them and she knows she and Reed would never live down a spontaneous moan, however innocent.

"You know what you need?" Reed says, still massaging. "You need a night away from home. Why don't you come over tonight and we can study for history?"

"Ugh! History!" Karyn says, dropping her head forward as Reed leans over to open the back door of the gym for her. "I totally forgot about that stupid test." The knots have already re-formed.

"Don't worry about it," Reed says. He pushes his hair back off his forehead as he moves away from the door toward the guys' locker room and walks backward so he can keep talking to her. "I already have a whole studying system thing down. We'll ace it."

"A whole studying system thing," Karyn repeats dryly, raising her eyebrows.

"Hey, what can I say, I'm a geek!" Reed says with a shrug. "So . . . my place tonight after practice? I'll bring the Double Stuf Oreos."

Karyn smiles her first real smile of the day. "I'm there," she says.

As Reed disappears into the locker room with the rest of the guys, Karyn finds herself fast forwarding to that evening. She's lying on her stomach on Reed's bed with her history notebook open in front of her. He's straddling his desk chair, constantly shooting a Nerf basketball while spouting out all the correct answers like he always does.

Maybe it's lame to look forward to a study session with her best friend, but at least it's *something* to look forward to—instead of sitting in the cold-war zone, ruminating about her mother's latest conquest and T. J. and his extracurricular activities. Yeah, a few hours chilling with Reed should be just the thing she needs.

"Awww! Are you thinking about T. J.?" Gemma's semi-sarcastic voice slices through Karyn's thoughts.

She flushes as her friends, none of whom have broken a sweat, file in through the back door. "No. Why?" Karyn says as she joins them on their way to the locker room.

"You were standing there all gooey eyed," Jeannie says. "If you weren't thinking about T. J., then I'd say he has some competition."

• • •

By the time Jeremy's eighth-period class comes to an end, he is ready to take off. Everyone knows. One thing he never anticipated in telling Tara the truth was the spurned girlfriend's need for vengeance. That and the fact that Tara's best friends are the biggest gossips in the school. In their worthy hands the news has taken less than three class periods to permeate the entire student body.

Jeremy cuts through the postschool mayhem in the hallways, trying not to notice that everyone is stopping to stare at him. He wishes with every fiber of his being that he'd never told Tara. He knows that she's hurt, but how could she do this to him? She has to know all of this is hard for him, too, but she just made it harder in order to make it easier for herself. In order to get sympathy. He feels like he never knew her at all.

There are no locker stops. No pauses at the water fountain. He is not, by any stretch of the imagination, going to football practice. He may be losing it, but it's not like he's feeling suicidal.

Jeremy pushes through the front doors of the school, and the fifty or so kids already waiting for their buses gradually turn to look at him—first the ones in the front, and then the ones in the middle, and finally the ones in the back. He spots his car across the lot and nothing has ever looked so welcoming to him in his life.

"Mandile!" a loud male voice calls.

Here it comes. Jeremy keeps walking, and the crowd parts for him. He feels like a cross between a rock star and a leper.

"Jeremy!"

He stops at the sound of Karyn's voice. Once he knows it's her, he realizes the first shout was from Reed. He can't shut them out. And he knows instinctively that they're not going to give him a hard time. At least he *thinks* he knows. Nothing seems to be the way he'd thought it was. He steels himself for the worst, just in case.

"Hey," Reed says as he and Karyn catch up with him on the edge of the parking lot, a few yards off from the still watching bus waiters. "Everything okay?"

Jeremy smiles sarcastically as a brisk wind blasts by and makes all the hairs on his neck stand up. He doesn't even have his jacket. "Yeah. Everything is great! I break up with my girlfriend and she runs around school telling everyone I'm gay. Couldn't be better!"

He's not sure why he's still itching to deny it. Habit? Desperate need to cling to his old life? Survival instinct? Not that it really matters. It's clear from the concerned, knowing look that Karyn and Reed share that neither one of them believes him. How is this possible? Have they always known he was gay? Has it somehow been that obvious? "Guys, she's just trying to get back at me," Jeremy says. But even to him it sounds halfhearted. He's tired. Ever since he's had to start actively lying about this, it's been wearing away at him. Three days and he's already exhausted. Too exhausted to keep hoping to *himself* that none of this is true. It's just impossible to avoid it anymore.

"If you need anything . . . ," Karyn says, trailing off quickly. Reed curls the brim of his cap and they look at each other again. Jeremy suddenly wants to scream at them. Tell them to stop with the looks. Stop with everything. This is *his* life! Why does everyone care so freakin' much about it?

He looks over at the crowd and about twenty people instantly turn away. Why can't they all just accept him for who he is . . . ? Or . . . was? Or . . . who he was always supposed to be? Why can't they just leave it alone?

Jeremy hears a car pull up behind him and a door slam. He's about to turn around when he hears a voice that makes his blood run cold.

"Jeremy . . . hey."

It's Josh. Reed and Karyn look past Jeremy, then look at each other once again. He knows what they're thinking. *Is this the guy?* The crowd in front of the school falls almost silent. Jeremy turns around slowly. *This is not happening. It can't be.*

But it is. Josh is standing there next to his car, smiling an easy smile. And just in case there's any confusion or doubt as to who he is, he's wearing a bright red-and-white Kennedy High School jacket. Jeremy waits to wake up. Actually stands there for a moment and wills himself to open his eyes and come out of this nightmare. But of course he doesn't. That only happens in movies.

Somehow he makes his shaky legs move. By the time he's face-to-face with Josh, the smile is gone from Josh's lips. He's staring at Jeremy's face, looking a bit less sure of himself. A bit nervous.

"What are you doing here?" Jeremy whispers. There are a million eyes boring into the back of his neck.

Josh's gaze flicks around, aware now that they have an audience. "I just came to say hi. See if you wanted to get something to eat or . . . something," he whispers back uncertainly. He pushes his hands into his pockets and squirms slightly, starting to understand that this just may have been a mistake.

Jeremy looks Josh directly in the eye. He knows his own eyes are full of anger, but he can't help it. What was Josh thinking, showing up here? Didn't he just *tell* him he wasn't sure what he was doing yet? Didn't he tell him he wasn't ready? He doesn't want this. He knows that now. He doesn't want to be out. And it's too late. There's nothing he can do to take it back. And none of it was his decision. His whole life has been obliterated and it's all Josh's fault. Josh and his stupid, unsolicited kiss.

"Get in the car," Jeremy says through clenched teeth. "Get in the car and drive away."

Josh's eyes are wide, but he stands his ground. "Jeremy, I could be a straight friend coming to pick you up. You don't have to make a big deal out of this."

All Jeremy can hear is condescension.

"Get the hell out of here," Jeremy says, his hands curling into fists. "Or I swear to God, you're going to regret it."

Josh's face falls, but he turns and gets into his car without a word and peels out. Jeremy doesn't even hesitate. He doesn't turn around to gauge the reaction of the Falls High student body or even to look at Reed and Karyn. All he can think about is getting to his car, turning on the radio, and screaming as loud as humanly possible.

• • •

"Never a dull moment around here," Jane says, sounding almost sad as she pushes Peter through the crowd that's just now breaking up after the Jeremy and Random Guy

128

sideshow. Everyone has a comment, and though Peter tries not to hear, he can't help but pick up a few as he moves through the clumps of legs and backpacks.

". . . *totally* gay . . ."

"Poor Tara . . . Do you think they . . ."

". . . no way! He's on the football team!"

"Maybe he and Reed Frasier . . ."

"Bite your tongue!"

Snickers. Laughs. Hands over mouths. Disbelieving eyes. Peter's disgusted. "Jane! Wait up!"

Peter's chair stops and he and Jane glance up to find Danny Chaiken jogging through the crowd toward them. He's wearing a yellow-and-black Charlie Brown T-shirt that makes him look like he's not a day older than thirteen. Peter could swear Danny's yearbook picture has looked exactly the same since seventh grade.

"What's up, man?" Danny says, giving Peter the chin-tilt acknowledgment common among guys who know each other but don't hang together. Peter notices that Danny's eyes don't even touch his chair. Most people look at it for a moment too long and then spend the next five minutes trying really hard to look like they never noticed it at all. Points for Danny.

"Jane, how long does this piece have to be?" Danny asks. He tucks his hands under his arms and rocks back and forth on his feet, heel to toe, heel to toe.

"About four to five minutes," Jane says, pushing her

hair behind her ears. "And don't hold back. The more intricate the better. I have to show them what I can do."

Danny's smile is so stiff, it seems drawn on. "Great. Yeah. No problem." He looks down at Peter. "So what'd you guys think of this afternoon's festivities? It's like, 'Tonight! On a very special WB movie. Jeremy Mandile. Is he . . . or isn't he?'"

Jane starts moving with a jerk, causing Peter's heart to jump in surprise. "I think it's sick the way everyone was standing around watching," she says.

Peter doesn't point out that he and Jane were two of those people. "Do you guys think he's gay?" he asks instead. His chair bumps around on the cracked concrete of the path that runs along the parking lot and he presses himself back into the chair, trying for stability.

"No way," Danny says, walking alongside Jane, hands still tucked. It gives the impression that he's in an invisible straitjacket. "If any of those guys on the football team were gay, the rest of the thumbheads would pound him. Jeremy would have been found in a Dumpster years ago."

Jane stops short and Peter has to grip the armrests to keep from flying forward.

"You know, you are one sick puppy," Jane says. Although she's behind Peter, he can imagine her angry, judgmental expression from the terseness in her voice.

"Chill, woman!" Danny says, holding up his hands in surrender and taking an exaggerated step back. He looks at

Peter and laughs as if to say, *You never know with these crazy girls.*

With another jerk Peter's on the move again, a lot faster this time. He sees his mom's car idling at the edge of the parking lot, the cloud from the exhaust puffing into the cold air.

"Personally, I couldn't care less whether or not the kid is gay," Jane says. "It's none of our damn business. And I think it sucks that everyone cares so much. What's the big damn deal? How does it affect them? It's his life. Is nothing sacred around here? I mean, what's next? Is the school newspaper going to print everyone's bra and jockstrap sizes? Can't we just live our own damn lives without everyone and their mother needing to know every detail?"

Peter presses his lips together, not quite sure how he's supposed to respond to her little tirade but sure that his body wants to burst out laughing. Somehow that doesn't seem appropriate. He glances up at Danny, and the second he sees the mirth he's trying to keep down as well, they both crack up. Jane stops and for a moment Peter is sure she's going to lace into them, but then her face softens and she laughs, too.

Danny pats her on the back of her shoulder. "You'd better cut down on the caffeine, girl," he says.

"Yeah, I think that's the most you've said to me since you became my trusty wheelchair driver," Peter puts in, relishing the pain in his stomach from laughing so hard.

He can't remember the last time he felt that. "I think you need a destressing massage or something."

Danny rubs his hands together. "At your service," he jokes, waggling his eyebrows at Jane.

"Hmmm . . . ," Jane says, bringing her index finger to her chin and looking up into the sky. "Let's see, I have to . . . go to jazz band practice, then catch the last hour of the Academic Decathlon meeting, then squeeze in half an hour working on the Web site before I head to TCBY, where I'll be partaking of a lovely meal of vanilla yogurt and pineapple for dinner." She glances back at Danny and smiles. Pete likes the way it looks on her and thinks she should do it more often. "If I can fit a massage in there somewhere, I'll give you a call."

"I think you need to put in a call to Overachievers Anonymous," Danny deadpans.

Jane chuckles, shaking her head, and together they walk Peter the rest of the way to his mother's car. After Peter says good-bye to Danny and Jane, he watches them walk off, going over everything that Jane has just said in his mind. For the first time in years, he realizes he feels kind of lucky.

Even though he's in a wheelchair and his parents are oblivious to the world, he could have it worse. At least he has no control over whether or not he ever walks again. Jane, Jeremy, and even Meena have to be feeling so much pressure. So much pressure to keep it up. Work harder and get into

Harvard. Deny everything and remain the heroic jock. Forget about whatever is making her miserable and be normal again.

There's no pressure on Peter because he has no control. He can't make himself walk again. It'll either happen or it won't.

Yep. I'm sure lucky, Peter thinks bitterly, his heart squeezing as his mother gets out of the car to help him in. Unfortunately, this particular kind of luck doesn't feel all that good.

CHAPTER EIGHT

"Hello, Jeremy!" Rita, the receptionist at the halfway house, is always a little bit too happy. Today her chipper voice grates on Jeremy's already frayed nerves the moment she opens her mouth. "You're not scheduled to work today."

"I know," Jeremy says shortly, earning an offended look from the receptionist. He's usually fairly tuned in to the feelings of everyone else around him, but tonight he barely even notices. "Is Josh here?"

Rita laughs and shakes her head. "Filing as usual," she says. "You poor kids must get so bored. . . ."

Jeremy is already out of the lobby and halfway up the steps before she can finish her sentence. He feels like his body is about to burst with anger and a tangled ball of other pent-up emotions. Confusion. Betrayal. Blame. Hurt. Misery. Guilt. He has to take this out. The punching bag in his basement didn't help. The shouting and singing at the top of his lungs in the car didn't help either.

If he doesn't release some of this soon, he's going to snap and drive into a brick wall. And that's not going to be good for anyone.

There is one person who deserves to be reamed right now. And screaming at him is the only thing Jeremy can imagine that will make him feel better. He swings open the door to the archive file room and Josh looks up from his work.

"Hey," Josh says tentatively. His hands clutch a folder as he stands up straight and looks Jeremy up and down, assessing the situation. Fittingly, his face registers concern.

"What were you thinking?" Jeremy whispers harshly. He knows his parents are out getting dinner because their car wasn't in the lot when he pulled up, but he still feels the need to keep it down. He takes a few steps into the room and leans on the table, where piles and piles of folders are stacked. Josh stands on the other side. "What did you do, wake up one morning and decide it would be fun to ruin my life?"

Josh's mouth drops open slightly and Jeremy is already starting to feel better. He wants more. More of these poisonous feelings out of his body.

"Are you kidding?" Josh says incredulously.

"Do I look like I'm kidding?" Jeremy spits out. He shoves himself away from the table, causing some of the piles of paper to teeter precariously. Josh jumps to steady them, but Jeremy just keeps venting. "I was fine. My life was fine. No . . . it was great. Everything was perfect until you invited me to that stupid party."

"Jeremy—"

"No one ever *asked* me if I wanted the world to know I'm gay. No one ever *asked* me if I wanted to be kissed," Jeremy blurts out, his voice unconsciously growing louder and louder. This feels so good, he wouldn't stop for anything. With each biting word, a little bit more of the tension in his veins is released. "No one ever asked me if I wanted to lose my girlfriend and have everyone in school talking about me. And tomorrow, I'm probably going to get my ass kicked. Did I ask for that? No. But thanks to you, I've got it all."

Jeremy raises his arms in the air in mock triumph and smiles sarcastically. "Thank you, Josh. You are my gayness guru. If I had been planning to come out, this is *exactly* the way I'd have wanted to do it."

Crossing his arms over the front of his cable-knit sweater, Josh comes around the table and faces Jeremy. His undeterred calm gets right under Jeremy's skin. "Are you done?"

"I'm just getting started," Jeremy says, mimicking Josh's cross-armed pose. "What the hell were you thinking, showing up at my school today?" he demands. "I just told you last night that I wasn't ready for all of this. Did you not hear that, or are you just in the habit of completely ignoring people?"

"I don't believe you," Josh says, taking a step back and letting out a sound through the back of his throat that's half laugh, half snort. "Look, like I said this afternoon, I just thought it would look like a friend meeting a friend. Which it would have if you hadn't freaked out and made a scene."

Jeremy narrows his eyes. "Great plan, Josh. Only one hitch. I broke up with Tara this afternoon, and by the time you made your little surprise visit, she'd pretty much made sure that everyone from the janitor to the backup kicker on the freshman football team knows that I'm gay. Actually, I believe *flamer* was the word I heard most often this afternoon. So there was basically no way your presence was going to look like anything but what it was."

Josh hangs his head. Scratches at the back of his neck. "I'm sorry," he says. "I . . . I didn't know."

"Well, now you do," Jeremy says. He turns to stalk out of the room, feeling like he's expelled all the negative energy he possibly can, and freezes dead in his tracks.

His parents are standing at the door. And from the devastated, shocked expressions on their faces, they've heard every word.

• • •

Karyn pulls her car to a stop in Reed's driveway on Thursday evening and flips down the visor. She does a quick check of her makeup in the lighted mirror and smiles. She's been looking forward to some bonding time with Reed all day and as an added bonus, her mother wasn't even home when she got back from practice, so she didn't have to worry about sneaking out. Her mom probably doesn't even remember that Karyn is grounded, but still, not having to deal with the cold shoulder helped Karyn relax a bit.

She gets out of the car, pulling her backpack with her, and strides up the walk, taking in a few deep breaths of the cold autumn air. As she reaches out to press the doorbell, her heart gives a little unexpected flutter of anticipation. What's that about?

Before she can consider the matter further, Karyn hears heavy footsteps approaching the door and can see Reed in her mind's eye, clad in sweatpants and his football T-shirt, jogging across the foyer to greet her. The door swings open and Karyn looks up to find—

"T. J.!" she blurts out, her heart giving a little extra-hard thump. She's so surprised to see him that she isn't even sure how she feels.

"Babe!" he exclaims. He wraps his strong arms around her and hugs her to him, crushing the buttons of her jacket into her chest and making her wince. "How did you know I was home?"

"I . . . uh . . ." Karyn's still gathering her thoughts when she feels her feet once again touch the ground. Suddenly her smile feels forced. As T. J. kisses her quickly on the lips, she realizes with a start that she's actually disappointed. She feels like a little cloud is settling over her, which doesn't make any sense at all. T. J.'s home. She should be psyched.

"So? You didn't answer my question!" T. J. says, holding both of her hands and grinning from ear to ear. It was amazing how both the Frasier boys got to be so big while still maintaining such an innocent-little-kid aura about them. "How did you know I was home? *I* was going to come over to your place and surprise *you*."

Karyn takes one look into T. J.'s excited blue eyes and gives herself a mental shake. This is her boyfriend. The guy she loves. The guy who has gone to obvious pains to get a close shave for her this evening and has even ironed his shirt. She should be nothing but happy to see him. She *is* happy to see him.

"Well, you know," she says flirtatiously, giving his huge hands a little squeeze. "*Everyone* knows when the great T. J. Frasier comes into town."

T. J. laughs and kisses her forehead, apparently satisfied with her nonanswer to his question. As he pulls her upstairs, Karyn's mind is still reeling. What is he doing here in the middle of the week? And why didn't she notice his car? Then she remembers. Reed's car was in the driveway, which means, of course, that T. J.'s precious Range Rover is in the garage, taking up the extra space. T. J.'s sparkly new auto always gets preference over Reed's hand-me-down Subaru Outback.

Karyn catches Reed's eye as she and T. J. get to the top of the plushly carpeted stairs. He's leaning against the door of his bedroom, arms crossed over his chest, legs crossed at the ankle. Blue sweats and his football T-shirt, just as Karyn predicted. She gives him a small smile, but he doesn't reciprocate.

"Hey," he says. "We still gonna study?" The resigned look in his eyes tells Karyn that he already knows the answer to this question, and she can't help but feel that there's a challenge there, too—like he's daring her to tell T. J. she has to study—that she's not actually here for him. Karyn and Reed both know she's not going to do that, but for a split second that challenge in Reed's eyes makes her want to, just to prove them both wrong. But T. J. came home to surprise her, and he's her boyfriend. That has to take precedence over some silly history test, right?

"Study, schmudy," T. J. says, wrapping his arms around Karyn's waist from behind and apparently not noticing the implication that she's here for Reed, not, in fact, for the great T. J. Frasier. "She hasn't seen her man in weeks."

With that, T. J. spins her around and Karyn lets out a little yelp/laugh as he carries her to his room. She manages to cast an apologetic look in Reed's direction before T. J. deposits her on his bed and closes the door.

"Hey, K.," T. J. whispers, sitting down next to her on

his double mattress and running a fingertip gently down her cheek.

"Hey, Teej," she says with a smile, her heart pounding for real as she combs her fingers through his spiky blond hair. She hasn't realized until this moment how much she's missed him—even the silly little ritual they go through each time they kiss.

As T. J. brings his lips to hers, she's struck for the hundredth time by how gentle he is with her even though he's this impossibly big guy. She wraps her arms around his neck and pulls him down onto the pillows. As she breathes in the minty scent of his aftershave and his hand runs over her sweater, under the hem, and onto her bare stomach, Karyn forgets all about studying, all about history, and all about Reed.

• • •

"Thanks, Norma," Meena says as Norma refills her coffee cup. She stares at her distorted reflection in the napkin holder she's twirling on the slick surface of the table in front of her. She closes one eye, and her lash line seems to spread out to four inches in the warped silver side of the little box.

"You don't have to thank me every time, hon," Norma says, topping off Meena's cup. She places one hand on her hip and snaps her gum. "It'd get old real fast."

The comment would sound rude if Meena didn't know better. Every sarcastic thing Norma says has a kindly smile behind it. Meena can't believe she's come to know this diner waitress so well that she can read into the way she talks.

"You gonna eat that pie I brought you?" Norma asks.

Meena glances at the slab of peach pie. The ice cream that was on top has long since melted into a thick pool around the slice and is dripping over onto the table. Meena didn't ask for it, and she feels neither hunger nor revulsion looking at it. She just knows she's not going to eat it. Lifting a fork seems like an alien notion.

"Doubt it," Meena says. Then, not wanting to sound obnoxious to the one person who is ever nice to her anymore, she adds, "But thanks."

Norma leans over Meena to pick up the plate, and the smell of mint gum and stale cigarette smoke curls into Meena's nostrils. She's come to find this scent comforting.

"A girl can dream," Norma says good-naturedly. Then she walks away, leaving Meena to her coffee. For the hundredth time since she's become a regular here, Meena says a silent thank-you for Norma's habit of never asking questions. She knows her presence here merits at least a few.

"Man! You are so busted!" someone shouts, following it up with a cackle. A loud burst of voices and laughter follows and Meena looks toward the other side of the diner. She notices the wheelchair first, then raises her eyes to see Peter Davis sitting at the end of a crowded table—the only member of a gang of guys who is not laughing. Even so, Meena instinctively knows it's not because he's the butt of the joke. It's obvious by his slumped posture and his less-than-enthused expression that he's just plain bored.

Almost as if he feels her watching, he looks over. The second he does, Meena finds a million things to study in her coffee cup. Is he going to come over here? Suddenly it seems like Peter Davis is everywhere, and she doesn't know what to make of it.

She sees him pull his chair away from the table. Max Kang shouts after him, asking him where he's going, and Meena knows he's coming to her. If it's more interesting company he's after, he's definitely not going to get it here.

Meena glances up and attempts a smile as Peter stops next to her booth. "Come here often?" he says, amusement in his eyes.

She pushes the smile a millimeter farther and looks down, letting her hair fall forward to cover her face. *If you only knew,* she thinks.

"How've you been?" Peter asks, his tone more serious. She sees his hands grip the ends of the armrests on his chair. His cuticles are all torn and some of them are bloody. Just like hers. But then, a guy in a wheelchair might have a lot to bite his nails over. She and Peter are, in a sense, both trapped. "I mean . . . you didn't seem so hot when I saw you in the nurse's office," Peter adds ten-

143

tatively, as if he's not sure at all if it's something he should bring up.

"Okay," Meena says, shrugging one shoulder. "I mean I . . . okay."

"Yeah?" Peter asks. He ducks his head, trying to see under the blanket of her hair.

She lifts her eyes and chin and the strands fall back slightly. "Yeah. I mean, since the fire . . . It hasn't been the *best* few days. . . ." She trails off, already feeling like she's said too much.

"Well, at least nothing can be worse than living through that . . . right?" Peter says, his eyes searching hers. For a moment she's reminded of her mother's penetrating gaze, but then she realizes this is different. Peter's bright green eyes are missing a quality she's seen in just about everybody else's for weeks. The disappointment isn't there. That's what it is. When people look at her—Dana, Luke, her parents—they have disappointment in their eyes. Like she's done something to let them down. She has, of course, but it's such a relief to talk to someone—even just to look at someone—who doesn't feel that.

"Right?" Peter repeats.

"Right," Meena answers. "Things can only get better." She just wishes she believed it.

• • •

As impossible as it seems, time stands still as Jeremy hovers in the middle of the archive room, his eyes locked

144

with the pleading eyes of his father. *Pleading* is the only word Jeremy can think to describe them. Pleading with Jeremy to say that none of what he's heard is true. But Jeremy can't deny any of it. It's too much to explain away. And the longer they stand there, the more the pleading seeps out of his father's eyes and is replaced by a hardness that makes Jeremy's blood run cold.

"Josh," his father says, never taking his eyes from Jeremy. "Would you excuse us, please?"

"Mr. Mandile, I hope you know—"

"Please, Josh," Jeremy's dad says. It's his no-nonsense voice. A person would have to be an idiot to argue with it. Jeremy knows from experience.

Josh, smart guy that he is, slips out of the room. Jeremy is left alone with his parents, his brain reeling. First everyone at school found out without him intending it, and now his parents have found out without him intending it.

Jeremy sits back carefully on the edge of the table, his whole body on alert as he watches his father walk slowly around the room. His dad's head is bent and his hand is over his mouth. Jeremy knows his dad is trying to find the right thing to say. His dad is big on always having the exact right thing to say. His mom, however, is a different story. Her face is blank as she stands like stone next to the door. Jeremy racks his brain for something to say to them. Anything that will make them understand what they just heard and make them okay with it, but he has no idea where to begin.

"What's going on, Jeremy?" his father says finally, stopping his pacing. His hand is still on his chin and his other hand is holding his elbow for support.

There's no point in denying anything. They heard it all. "Well, this obviously isn't the way I wanted to tell you guys," Jeremy says, looking from his mother to his father and back again, his heart slamming away in his chest. Actually, he didn't even *want* to tell them at all. "But it turns out I'm gay." He almost laughs at how silly that sounds. "It doesn't turn out I'm gay. I'm gay." It sounds so weird to actually say it out loud. It's real now. Unavoidable. *I'm gay.* It's such a happy-sounding word for something that feels so hard to say aloud.

"Are you *smiling?*" his father demands so loudly, it makes Jeremy start. "Is this *funny* to you?"

Jeremy can't believe what he's hearing or what he's seeing. His father's face is bright red and contorted with anger. Over the past few days he's thought about telling his parents. He knew they'd be surprised, but he'd always thought they'd be calm, levelheaded, reasonable, and accepting. After all, his parents are the most liberal people he knows. They deal with drug addicts, runaways, alcoholics, and any number of other messed-up people every single day and all the while preaching acceptance to their kids. His father can't really be yelling at him for coming to grips with who he really is. Can he?

"Dad, I—"

"This is no laughing matter, Jeremy," his father says, taking a few steps toward him. Jeremy can practically feel the heat of his father's anger coming off him in waves. "You have been lying to me and to your mother. You have been hiding this from us for God knows how long. How could you be so deceitful?"

"Tony, please," Jeremy's mother says, taking one tentative step away from the wall. Then she seems to think better of it and steps back, too shaky to support herself. "Don't yell."

"I'll yell if I want to!" Jeremy's father roars. "This is ridiculous, Jeremy. No. You are too young to know this about yourself. You've been dating Tara for two years! Are you about to tell me that you have no feelings for her? That you're not attracted to her?"

Jeremy struggles to find his voice before his father continues his tirade. "I . . . I thought I was, but I—" His voice keeps cracking and he stops. He hates how pathetic he sounds, but he can't help it. These can't be his parents. They can't really be reacting like this.

"You're not gay," his father says. He stands directly in front of Jeremy, his bulky frame intimidating as he looks Jeremy in the eye for the first time since Josh left the room. "You're just confused, Jeremy. That's all this is. Josh somehow got to you and you're confused. You're not gay."

Jeremy blinks a few times at his father, trying to process what he's just said. Make some sense out of it. But the words don't rearrange themselves into anything approaching coherent. They're as absurd as Jeremy now realizes his own thoughts were when he tried to rationalize himself out of accepting the truth. Hearing Josh call him a gay person felt strange, but hearing his dad say that he *isn't* gay—it feels flat-out wrong.

But his father is going way beyond confusion here. He's actually accusing Josh of messing with Jeremy's head and trying to make him believe he's gay. His father is actually implying that Jeremy has a choice in the matter. Like Jeremy would really choose a lifestyle that would make him a target and cause his whole existence to be a struggle. Why does he think Jeremy's been hiding this anyway? For *fun?*

"I can't believe this," Jeremy says slowly. His voice comes out as a cracked whisper.

"What?" his father demands, his eyes practically popping out of his head.

"I said, I can't believe this," Jeremy repeats. He pushes himself away from the table and stands up straight, happy that he's got a couple of inches on his dad. "You guys have known repeat-offense crack addicts who you've treated like members of the family. But your only son tells you he's gay and you act like I've joined a cult or something. Like Josh has some kind of voodoo mind trick going on me and all I need is a good shake to snap out of it. What happened to all your preaching about acceptance? About loving everyone for who they are?" Jeremy's close to tears and he hopes his father doesn't notice. The last thing he needs is to have a bawling breakdown.

"Don't you throw our jobs in our faces," Jeremy's father shouts, pointing a finger at Jeremy's chest and making him take a step back, much to his chagrin. "This is different. You are our flesh and blood. This is not the life I want for my only son. And what about your sister? Have you even thought about the example you're going to set for Emily?"

"Emily," Jeremy's mother says. The first word she's uttered in at least five minutes. When Jeremy looks at her, he finds that she's actually wringing her hands. Up until now he'd always thought that was just an expression. "I'm so glad I got a sitter for her tonight. I don't know how I'll explain this to her. . . ."

His mother's voice stumbles on the last word and she starts to weep quietly. Jeremy's heart breaks. He hates to see his mother cry. And to know he caused it makes the pain run that much deeper. But what hurts more than anything is the fact that she can't even look at him. The fact that she's not even trying to understand.

Jeremy takes a deep breath and pulls himself up straight. It's hard with all the sadness and disappointment weighing him down, but he manages. He looks at his father and feels like he doesn't recognize the man standing before him.

"I don't even know you," Jeremy says slowly, somehow managing to keep his voice even. "Everything you've ever told me . . . everything you've ever stood for is a lie."

Jeremy's father takes a loud, deep breath through his nose, his nostrils flaring. "I will not be spoken to that way," he says. "And I don't feel there's anything more to say here, unless you want to apologize."

But apologizing is the last thing Jeremy has on his mind right now. He's too busy dealing with the fact that his parents are completely different people than he always thought they were.

After staring him down for a few seconds, waiting for the words he's not going to hear, Jeremy's father turns and walks out of the room, slamming the door behind him.

Jeremy sinks down into the folding chair and covers his face with his hands. Everyone hates him. Tara. Josh. His mother. His father. It's only taken three short days for his entire world to come crashing down around him. Without a word, his mother slowly follows his dad, closing the door behind her with a quiet click. Jeremy's heart twists painfully in his chest and he finally lets himself cry.

He feels like they've just closed the door on him forever.

CHAPTER NiNE

Friday morning, Jeremy lies in bed, his flannel sheets folded neatly at his waist, his hands folded on his stomach. He stares, dry-eyed, at the glow-in-the-dark Star Wars stickers he plastered to his ceiling when he was ten years old. Back then, a lot of his friends weren't even aware of what Star Wars was, but his father had sat him down and watched all three videos with him on successive Sunday afternoons. He'd told Jeremy that if there was one thing he wanted to impart to his son, it was a love of Star Wars. Jeremy smiles sadly as he remembers how much he loved those Sundays. Just him and his dad sitting in the darkened den, scarfing popcorn as his father explained the intricacies of the whole dark side/force relationship. Back then, Jeremy couldn't imagine loving anyone more than he loved his father.

Now he's not even sure if his father will ever speak to him again.

When Jeremy pushes himself out of bed, his whole body

protests. There wasn't much sleep going on in this room last night. Just thinking. Worrying. Dreading. Sleeping was a scientific impossibility. The second he's up, Pablo is up as well, but Jeremy is so out of it, the jangle of the dog's tags surprises him. Pablo shoves his cold nose into Jeremy's palm, wagging his tail like crazy.

Jeremy squats to scratch behind Pablo's ears. "Good boy," Jeremy says as Pablo wags faster. "You still love me, huh?" He kisses the dog on top of his head. Pablo gives Jeremy's face a couple of quick licks and Jeremy grimaces, then smiles. "Yeah, you'll always love me," he says, and his heart actually gives a pathetic little squeeze. Jeremy stands quickly and lets the dog out of the room before he starts blubbering something about man's best friend.

As Jeremy dresses, he realizes it's Friday. Which means that there's a game tomorrow. Which means that he's supposed to wear his football jersey to school today. Isn't that ironic? He'll be wearing the very same clothes as the guys who are undoubtedly going to track him down and try to beat him to a pulp. Jeremy's stomach turns when he thinks of what Mike Chumsky might have to say to him. What he and his pals on the football team might want to do to him. He pulls his jersey over his head and stares at himself grimly in the mirror. Maybe going to school today is not such a good idea.

Letting out a huge yawn, Jeremy walks out of his room and over to the top of the stairs. His pulse is starting to race and he realizes that he's afraid to see his parents. Afraid of what verbal slams his dad might serve up to him this morning. He pauses, his hand gripping the top of the banister as he strains to hear if anyone is talking in the kitchen. All he hears is the faintest tinkling sound of silverware against dishes. Taking a deep breath, Jeremy trudges down the stairs.

He finds Emily alone at the breakfast table, eating from a huge bowl of Froot Loops. No juice. No toast. No warm food of any kind. This is a new one. His mother almost always makes a hot breakfast. Jeremy falls into a chair. Apparently she isn't up to cooking this morning.

"Good morning," Emily says. She smiles up at him as she wipes a drop of milk from her chin with the back of her hand. Just that small smile touches Jeremy so deeply, he can't believe it. At least someone in this family still likes him. Someone besides Pablo, anyway.

"Where's Dad?" Jeremy asks, reaching for the cereal box even though he's not remotely hungry. He glances at the empty chair his father usually occupies as if it's going to strike out and bite him.

"He left for work early," Emily says. Then she leans forward, her red hair framing her wide eyes. "And mom isn't even *dressed* yet," she says in a conspiratorial whisper.

Wow. That *is* a big deal. Jeremy reaches into the box and grabs a few pieces of dry cereal. But as soon as he pops them into his mouth, his stomach churns and he knows it was a mistake. He forces himself to chew and swallow.

"Did you guys have a fight?" Emily asks, laying her little hands flat on top of the Formica table.

Jeremy winces. He can't lie to her. And there's no point in it, anyway. "Yeah," he says, folding his arms on the table and resting his chin on top of them so he's closer to her height.

"Really?" Her eyes are wide, as if she's surprised to have guessed correctly. "About what?"

Jeremy hesitates. He doesn't want to say anything to Emily that would cause the rift between him and his parents to widen. "They . . . don't like one of my friends," he says finally, thinking of Josh. It's not *that* far off from the truth. If they really believe Josh somehow brainwashed him into being gay, then they're none too happy with the guy right now.

"You're kidding. All of your friends are so cool!" Emily says.

This brings a true smile to Jeremy's face. He's always loved how Emily looks up to him and his friends, following them around and copying the girls' styles. But then he recalls what his father said the night before about setting an example for Emily, and it's like someone's taken a wrecking ball to his gut. Sooner or later Emily is going to find out he's gay. What will she think? What if she doesn't understand or is ashamed of him? In a perfect world, Emily would still love him and be proud of him. But after the way his parents reacted . . .

Before Jeremy can finish his thought, his mother walks into the room, her hair in a messy bun and her bathrobe tied loosely at her waist. She glances at Jeremy but says nothing as she heads for the coffeemaker.

Jeremy swallows hard. "Guess it didn't feel like a pancake morning," he jokes, attempting to alleviate the tension she's brought with her into the room.

"Well, thanks to certain people I kind of have a lot on my mind this morning, Jeremy," she snaps.

Jeremy takes her comment as the slap in the face she means it to be but surprises even himself when he abruptly stands up, ready to snap right back at her. He hadn't realized until this moment how much fight he has in him. How ready and willing he is to stand up for himself. That he's actually started to accept the facts about himself after denying them for so long.

But one look at the trepidation on his sister's face makes him think better of it. His mother looks at him warily, as if she'd expected no response. Well, she's not getting one for now, but Jeremy doesn't like the implication that he's somehow done something to her.

"We'll talk later," he tells her, looking her dead in the eye so she knows he means it. He's not going to take this much longer. He's the one who deserves some support around here, and he can't be treated like he's some kind of enemy just because he's being honest about himself.

Jeremy tells Emily to have a good day at school and walks out of the house, shaking all the way. The anger he's feeling now actually feels kind of good—better than the shame, disappointment, and shock cocktail he was feeling last night.

But when he gets to the driveway, he takes one look at his car and realizes he has nowhere to go. He doesn't want to go to school. He turns and looks at the front door of his house. But he definitely can't go back in there right now.

Jeremy takes a deep breath and holds it in his chest for a moment, allowing the fresh air to fill him up.

"Might as well get this over with," he tells himself.

Letting his responsible side take over, Jeremy gets in his car and heads for Falls High. As much as he'd like to, he knows he can't avoid school forever.

• • •

"Thank God it's Friday!" Keith Kleiner exclaims, throwing his hands in the air in a praise-the-Lord gesture and tilting his head back so fast, his glasses fly off and fall to the linoleum floor behind him.

"Keith, you are such a tool," Max says as his friend stops to scoop up his glasses and blow the dirt from the lenses.

Peter is only half paying attention to his friends' antics as Doug pushes his wheelchair through the lobby. He's just noticed Meena ducking her way into school, her tangled hair hiding her face. She pushes past a group of cheerleaders, all decked out in uniform in their weekly day-before-a-game tradition, and they glare at her like she's some kind of troll. The contrast is striking. Meena in her dirty, dark clothes she's been wearing for at least the last twenty-four hours, Gemma Masters and crew in their bright blue-and-gold pleats with their faces perfectly painted on.

Peter thinks Meena is still more striking than any of them.

He watches Meena dodge and weave her way through the crowd and recalls their minute-long conversation the night before. It's clear that something is going on with her. A few months ago she would have been standing with those cheerleaders, tossing her hair with the best of them. Now she won't look anyone in the eye and has obviously not seen a shower in days. And it can't just be because of the fire. In fact, Peter seems to remember that the change had started in her weeks ago. He is struck with the urge to follow her. To just talk to her again. He wants to see her return to the land of the living even if it's only for one more minute.

Plus it doesn't hurt that talking to Meena was one of the only times he's completely forgotten that he's stuck in this stupid chair.

Peter glances up at Doug, who has stopped to talk to a few of his burnout friends, and wonders if he can wheel himself away without Doug noticing. The last thing he needs is the predictable mock-fest he'll have to endure for going to talk to a girl. In the area of guy-girl relationships, Peter's friends haven't matured much past the "Ew! You're talking to a *girl!*" phase of the second grade. Max and Keith are busy discussing the nuances of the latest MxPx album, so they aren't about to say anything. Peter realizes that if he's going to do this, he should probably seize the moment.

Taking the wheels in his hands, Peter starts off. Meena has stopped at her locker, so she's not going anywhere for a couple of minutes. But the second he moves, Peter rethinks this whole idea. What if she blows him off? What if talking to her twice in two days is tantamount to annoying her? With her hunched shoulders and her hair curtain, she's not exactly giving off a social vibe.

"Dude, what're you looking at?" Doug says, effectively bursting Peter's bubble. He squeezes his eyes shut as Doug looks down the hallway for anything that might be worthy of Peter's attention. "Are you staring at the weird girl?"

This last question and its delighted tone get the attention of Keith and Max, who both squint at Meena, who is, mercifully, too far away to hear. "Classic!" Keith declares. "Peter is in love with the weird girl."

"Don't call her that," Peter says through his teeth before he can think better of it. His three friends' faces register total glee.

"Ooooh! Defensive!" Doug says, bringing his hands together over his heart dramatically. "It *is* love!"

"If I want to hang out with five-year-olds, I can go back to kindergarten," Peter says, leveling them with a glare. He jerks the wheels of his chair backward and executes his very first perfect turn. The timing couldn't have been better. He moves away from his so-called friends as fast as his wheels will carry him, which is pretty fast with his arms working on such an adrenaline rush.

"Ow! Hit us where it hurts!" Keith yells after him sarcastically. A burst of laughter follows and Peter feels a flush of anger and embarrassment take over his face.

Meena's gone by the time he passes her locker, but he's no longer in the frame of mind to talk to her, anyway. All he can think about is seriously reconsidering his choice of friends.

• • •

As Jeremy cuts through the hallway toward his locker on Friday morning, he feels like he's walking through a horror movie and he's the swamp monster. Or at least the swamp monster's most recent, disfigured victim. Each little clutch of people he passes stops just before he gets to them and gapes. Then they cover their mouths and whisper. Like he really doesn't know they're talking about him.

The moment Jeremy turns out of the main hallway, his heart stops beating. There are at least twenty people gathered around his locker, staring at it. A pair of junior girls who are dressed in head-to-toe black stand back from the rest, looking horrified. A few guys he barely knows are laughing so hard, they need to slap each other's backs. Jeremy stiffens and keeps walking. The moment someone spots him, everyone backs up, but no one walks away.

Finally Jeremy can see what has grabbed their attention. His locker is dented in the center, and spray painted down the front of the door in an angry red scrawl are three capital letters.

F-A-G.

Jeremy's whole body turns to liquid. Why is this happening? How can this possibly be fair? He takes a look around at his gawkers and each of them looks away as he catches their eyes. They can't possibly know how he feels right now. If they did, they wouldn't want to witness it. Would they?

He turns his back to them and starts on his combination. His neck is as hot as a stove coil. The inside of his locker is untouched. Ironic, since Jeremy looks fine from the outside, but inside he's a complete wreck.

Suddenly what little noise there is in the hallway gives way to complete silence. Jeremy hears a familiar squeak—sneaker rubber against linoleum—and looks up to find five guys coming toward him through the crowded hallway. Willis Hauer, Shaheem Dobi, Reed Frasier, Bobby Scorella, and, of course, Mike Chumsky. Their faces are grim. Jeremy grips the top of his locker door, the edge of the metal cutting into his skin. More than anything at this moment, he feels disappointment. He knew this was coming, but he never would have thought Reed would be involved.

The spectators back off a bit to give the new participants in Jeremy's little drama some space. He swears he sees some of their faces light up at this development in the train wreck of his life. Turning his back to the wall, Jeremy pulls himself up straight, his arms down at his sides, his fists clenched. He looks squarely at his friends.

"I guess this is where I get my ass kicked," he says. He may be a little bit scared, but his tone is thick with disdain. At least in this situation he knows he's the better man. He would never really threaten someone because he was different.

Reed is the first to speak. "Actually, I was thinking we would kick the ass of whoever did this to your locker."

Jeremy blinks. He instinctively looks at Mike Chumsky, whose face betrays his surprise. Still, Jeremy's stance relaxes the tiniest bit. Reed hasn't been seduced by the dark side.

"Isn't this cozy?" Tara's voice cuts through the hallway.

She walks up to Jeremy and the other guys, flanked by her best friends, Aggie Driver and Taline Aharonian. Jeremy can't help but notice that Tara looks amazing, even if her expression is all about vengefulness and hate. Wearing a low-cut brown sweater and more makeup than usual, she's obviously doing the postbreakup dress-to-kill thing.

"Guess what?" Tara says, looking Jeremy dead in the eye. "Aggie was at a certain Kennedy High party last weekend, and do you know what she saw?" Tara is loving this. Jeremy can't believe this is the same girl he's been with for almost two years. "She saw *you* kiss Josh Strauss. She didn't tell me until after we broke up because she didn't want to be a snitch, but I guess now it's your word against hers. Oh! And the Web site and Josh's appearance yesterday. Or did he just show up here to drive you to work?"

Jeremy glances at Aggie, who's practically purple from embarrassment. "I'm sorry," she mouths from behind Tara's back.

"So what do you have to say for yourself?" Tara asks, raising one eyebrow. "Still gonna deny it?"

Without hesitation, Reed steps away from the rest of the guys and stands next to Jeremy, facing Tara. "Go away, Tara," Reed says, leveling her with a glare. Her face colors and she opens her mouth, but Reed cuts her off. "Now. Before you say something that'll make you look worse than you already do."

Tara's face falls and she turns on her heel to stalk away. The bell rings and the crowd moves off slowly. It seems no one wants to miss what might come next. Finally Jeremy is left alone with his teammates. Apparently these guys don't care if they're late for class.

"So it's true, man?" Mike says, his face pure disgust. "You really are a fag?"

Jeremy looks at Reed and Reed just looks right back. The encouragement and support in his friend's eyes is all he needs at that moment.

"Yeah, it's true," Jeremy says. "Do you have a problem with that?"

Mike's jaw clenches. "Yeah, maybe I do."

Shaheem breaks away from the other guys and stands on Jeremy's other side, opposite Reed. The toothpick Shaheem constantly has in his mouth rolls around between his teeth.

"If you have a problem with him, then you've got a problem with me and Reed, too, man," he says. Jeremy watches as Mike's eyes travel over Shaheem's three-hundred-plus-pound linebacker frame and stop for a second on the toothpick that always seems to make the guy more threatening. Then he glances left and right at Willis and Bobby, none too shabby athletes themselves.

"It's still three against three," Mike says. His eyes are trained on Jeremy now. "And you've got a *girl* on your side." Jeremy feels his face flush and hates himself for it.

"You're such a moron, Chumsky," Reed says, smiling and shaking his head casually as if there isn't a throw down about to happen. Maybe Reed knows something Jeremy doesn't, because he has a feeling Mike is not going to back down. Not as long as he thinks he has a chance.

"Bobby. What the hell are you doing?" Shaheem says, glaring at his best friend. Bobby shifts his considerable weight from foot to foot and runs his hand over his blond hair. "You really gonna back up this loser instead of sticking with the guy you've been friends with since your potty-training days?"

Bobby glances at Jeremy, uncertain, but in the end his conscience wins out. He ducks his head and stands with Shaheem.

"You still wanna go?" Shaheem asks, crossing his arms over his chest as he looks down his nose at Mike. "'Cuz you know I'm *always* ready."

Glancing at Willis, Mike falters a bit and takes a step back, still glaring at Jeremy. He's obviously conflicted over whether to back down and lose the pain-free way or to stay and get his butt handed to him. Finally he scoffs and walks off with Willis trailing behind him.

"They're all freakin' fags, man," Mike says as he reaches the end of the hallway. Willis laughs loudly, and then they're gone.

It isn't until Jeremy lets out his breath that he realizes he's been holding it. "Thanks, you guys," he says weakly, feeling suddenly exhausted. "I mean . . . really Thanks."

"It's no problem," Reed says, holding his hand out flat palm up. Jeremy clasps his hand down into it and they quickly shake.

"So, man," Shaheem says, clapping an immense hand on Jeremy's shoulder. "I hear you got some action last weekend."

Shaheem grins and Jeremy and Reed both laugh. Jeremy glances over at Bobby, who's hanging back, smiling uncertainly. It's obvious that Bobby is uncomfortable with this whole scenario, but at least he stood by their friendship. And that's all Jeremy needs at this point. Some people to stand by him.

"You guys wanna go to the office and report this?" Shaheem asks, lifting his chin at Jeremy's vandalized locker.

As he slams the locker door shut, Jeremy realizes that he's physically spent—as if he *has* just gotten the crap kicked out of him. All he can envision in his mind's eye is his bed and his pillow.

"I think I'm just gonna go to the nurse and sign out," he says. "I didn't exactly sleep last night."

"Yeah, you look like crap, Mandile," Reed says jokingly, lifting his baseball cap and running his hand through his red hair before replacing it.

"All right. We'll report it," Shaheem says, chewing on his toothpick. "We'll see you at the game tomorrow, man."

He holds out his hand to Jeremy, who shakes it just as he did Reed's. As he walks off toward the office, he knows this whole thing is in no way over, but with guys like Reed and Shaheem and Bobby behind him, maybe it won't be as bad as he thought.

• • •

"Are you kidding me?" Karyn exclaims, one hand gripping the top of her locker door. Reed has just finished telling her the story of what happened between Jeremy and the rest of the guys that morning, and Karyn's whole body seems to be coursing with anger. "I can't believe Mike and Willis did that." She reaches up to pull a few notebooks out of her locker and envisions Mike and Willis's faces laughing maniacally. She's surprised by how easily the image conjures itself up in her mind. "Wait a minute," she says. "Yes, I can."

Reed shrugs one shoulder and shoves his hands into the front pockets of his jeans. "Yeah, well, it's not too surprising from Mike," he says. "I mean, we hang out with him, but he's always been kind of a moron."

Karyn snorts a laugh. There are certain people she is

not going to miss once the graduation caps have been tossed this June. In fact, if she could somehow do away with Mike Chumsky right now, she'd be quite happy, but she has a feeling Mr. Underachiever isn't exactly a candidate for early graduation. She can't believe she's actually hung out with a guy who would treat people like that.

"What are you thinking?" Reed asks. She doesn't have to look at him to know that his light eyebrows are coming together in concern.

"Nothing," Karyn says harshly. She pulls her monstrous math book down and shoves it so hard into her bag, she sends it flying out of her grasp. Her backpack hits the floor and her stuff comes spilling out over Reed's feet.

"I got it," Reed says, crouching to the floor and gathering up her books.

Karyn presses her eyes closed and shakes her head. *Get a grip,* she tells herself. *You're acting like a total spaz.* She looks down and is about to thank Reed for his chivalry when she sees his hand slowly reaching for a little blue box that's lying on top of her English notebook. A little blue box she hadn't taken out of her bag because she hadn't yet thought of a good hiding place for it in her bedroom. Karyn holds her breath, realizing there's no way he's going to just shove it into her bag without realizing what it is.

Reed picks up the box and seems to be studying it for an excruciatingly long time. Karyn stares down at the top of his baseball cap and wonders what he's thinking. And why is he just staring at it like that? And why do the words *reservoir tip* suddenly look so impossibly large?

Finally he looks up at her, still holding the box. His face is ashen. His freckles even look pale. Karyn's eyes lock with Reed's and she knows he has a million questions, the most prominent of which is written all over his face. *Are you having sex with my brother? Are my best friend and my brother having sex?*

When Reed's face suddenly clears, Karyn knows he's come to a conclusion. *Of course they're having sex. They've been together since May. What did you think they were doing all this time, hosting knitting circles?*

Even though she knows that once Reed gets over the initial shock of the thought of her in bed with his brother, he should be fine, something in his face tells her this isn't so. She can't pinpoint what it is, but Karyn is suddenly struck with the urgent desire to tell him he's wrong. That he's jumped to the wrong conclusion. That she and T. J. have not done the deed. But it's all too awkward. She and Reed never talk about her and T. J. They talk about everything but. And this doesn't feel like the right moment to delve into it.

Reed tosses the box into her bag, stands up, shoves the whole backpack into her hands, and walks away. That's it. No questions. No good-bye. No nothing.

For a few seconds Karyn just stands there, allowing her pulse to slow down and her brain to try to process what just happened. Why was she so compelled to deny everything?

Sure, she and T. J. aren't having sex, but there's no real harm in Reed thinking they are. It's perfectly natural and will probably happen sooner or later. In fact, sooner is looking more like a possibility now that Karyn has broken the condom-buying barrier. So why is Reed so thrown?

Karyn leans back against the lockers next to hers and recalls Reed's expression. Then, like a slice to the heart, she realizes what it was. Reed wasn't just shocked that she might be having sex with T. J., he was . . . jealous. Her stomach turns and squeezes, turns and squeezes, and Karyn immediately regrets the buttered bagel she had for breakfast. Is this possible? Is Reed actually jealous of T. J.? Could he actually have feelings for Karyn?

CHAPTER TEN

After a seriously long, seriously deep nap, Jeremy lies on top of his covers, Pablo curled up next to him, thinking over everything that has happened in the past couple of days. Jane showing him the Web site. Josh's understanding at the diner. Telling Tara the truth. Josh showing up at school. Ripping Josh apart the night before. The scene in the hallway that morning.

But what he keeps coming back to is his parents. The way they reacted was the one thing that Jeremy never could have predicted. And that's why it's the one thing that makes him feel the most let down.

The phone rings and Jeremy glances at the answering machine sitting on his desk. After three rings it picks up. Then Karyn starts to talk.

"Hey, Jeremy! It's me, Karyn. Listen, I just wanted you to know that everyone is actually being really cool about this whole thing. I mean . . . yeah . . . people are talking about it . . . but everyone is with you. I mean, everyone I've talked to, anyway. I guess what I'm saying . . . badly . . . is that you don't have to be worried about coming back to school. Those guys who did that to your locker are just losers. So, sorry for rambling. Hopefully I'll see you tonight. Bye."

Tonight, Jeremy thinks, listening to the dial tone that follows. Tonight is the big Halloween party. The one he was supposed to go to with Tara in some coupley costume. Jeremy wonders what will happen if he shows. If people will really be as cool as Karyn seems to think they are. He takes a deep breath and lets it out slowly. When it comes right down to it, Chumsky and Willis were the only ones at school who have said anything remotely off-color to him. (And Tara, of course, but she has reason to hate him.) Most people have stayed out of his face.

In fact, when he really thinks about it, the people who have treated him the worst are his parents. His liberal-edict-spouting parents.

Rolling over onto his side, Jeremy looks out the window at the cloudless sky. His mom and dad should be coming home within the next couple of hours. What is he going to do when they get there? He's not sure he can handle seeing their disappointed faces again. He knows that his news was unexpected and that, on some level, they do have the right to be disappointed. He's their only son, and it doesn't look like he's going to be giving them grandkids.

But shouldn't their love for him outweigh the loss of something that might never have happened, anyway?

With a loud sigh, Jeremy resolves to try to talk to his parents again. They've had twenty-four hours to take this in. To deal with it. To talk it through with each other. Maybe now they'll be ready to sit down and have a rational conversation with him.

Jeremy closes his eyes and sends a little prayer out into the cosmos. A little backup never hurts.

• • •

Friday afternoon, Danny leans up against the cool cinder block wall in the bathroom and glances for the fifth time in two minutes at his digital watch. Twenty-seven seconds. In twenty-seven seconds he'll duck out of the bathroom and into his music theory classroom just in time for the bell to ring. Good old Vega always starts class right on time. Jane won't have even half a second to accost Danny and ask him for an update. Danny's been doing this all week since Jane first asked him to do the piece. Last one in the door. First one out.

Five, four, three, two . . . one.

Danny reaches over and swings open the heavy wooden door. He can't help but smile. At least he hasn't lost his stealth abilities.

Of course, the moment he sees Jane waiting outside the music theory classroom door, the smile fades. Danny pauses, gripping his music composition notebook tighter.

He's too far from the bathroom to duck back in. Any second she's going to turn her head and see him. God! What is she doing out there? Is she actually waiting for him? What is she, the Gestapo? She asked him for a favor. Where does she get off keeping tabs on him?

But Danny knows he's trapped. And he knows he wouldn't have been hiding all week if he didn't feel like Jane has the right to be after him. There's nothing left to do but talk to her.

"Hey," he says, his shoulders slumping as he approaches the door. *Where's the bell?* he wonders. *Come on, bell. Any second now.*

"Hey," Jane says with a smile, pushing herself away from the wall. Her foot is tapping a psychotic beat. "How's the piece coming?"

She looks hopeful and desperate at the same time. What can Danny do but lie?

"Great!" he says. He lifts his composition notebook and smiles a bit too hard. "Almost done."

Jane's eyes zero in on the notebook like she's a starving dog and it's a big pile of steak. Realizing his mistake, Danny immediately brings his arm back down to his side, tucking the book just slightly behind his back. *Don't ask. Just don't,* he silently demands.

But she does. "Is that it?" Her voice is a couple of octaves too high. "Can I see it?" She makes a grab, and Danny has to turn sideways to pull far enough away from her.

"Not until it's done!" he says, managing to fumble out a light little laugh. As if she's *so* ridiculous to think he'd ever show her an unfinished piece. "I'm an *artiste*," he says in a tone that's half joking, half serious. "You'll have it when it's done."

The bell rings. "Thank God!" Danny mutters. Jane flicks her eyes over him like she's considering his sanity. *Smart girl*, Danny thinks.

"All right," she says. "But I need it soon. I have to get those tapes out." Ever the goody-goody, she glances over her shoulder at the classroom door as if she's waiting for Mr. Vega to come out and scold them. "And thanks again for doing this," she says, making Danny feel like a total scab. "I'll repay you by . . . I don't know . . . I'll pay for your next piercing or something," she says, glancing at the silver stud in his ear.

Danny snorts a fake laugh and raises his chin at her. "Good one!"

She makes a move to go into class, but Danny stays rooted to the spot. "You coming?" she asks, raising her eyebrows.

"I'll be right in," Danny answers.

The second she's through the door, Danny leans back against the row of lockers behind him. He tips his head forward and yanks it back, slamming his head into the metal so hard, he's sure he's left a dent.

"Nope. Nothing," he says to himself, marveling once

more at the complete numbness that now seems to be dulling his tactile senses as well.

He looks up at the ceiling and holds his breath, wishing he'd never said yes to Jane. Wishing he'd never written the piece that got her thinking he was some kind of musical genius. Wishing he'd never been born.

He knows he's not going to be able to write anything for her. Not like this. It's ironic, actually. The one time anyone has counted on him for anything and he's going to screw it up. But not because he's in one of the states this medication is supposed to help him avoid. In fact, in one of those states, he'd be a hell of a lot more useful to Jane Scott. If his mind wasn't being messed with like this, he's sure he'd write something brilliant.

But no. He's going to screw it up because some quack doctor is trying to cure him. And as Danny stands alone in the silent hallway, a bump he can't feel forming on the back of his head, he realizes what's actually happening here. What the doctor is actually trying to cure him of.

He's trying to cure Danny of himself. And the scariest part is—it's working.

• • •

He can tell. I know he can tell. He knows. He knows what I am. Everyone knows. I have to get out of here. I have to get out.

As Meena sits in the middle of the couch in Dr

174

Lansky's office on Friday afternoon, she hugs her legs to her chest. The last time she was here, she'd said virtually nothing to the gray man, and today isn't going to be any different. There are just a few problems with that theory—Meena is so hopped up on caffeine and sugar, she can't stop her thoughts from racing. She is absolutely petrified that at any moment her mental diarrhea is going to become verbal and she'll say something that she doesn't want to say. And once that happens, there will be no turning back.

"Meena, when was the last time you ate?" Dr. Lansky asks, leaning forward in his chair. He casts a doctorly look over her face, his eyes briefly resting on the dark circles under her own.

Ate! Ha! That's funny, Meena thinks. All she's consumed in the last forty-eight hours is Coke, coffee, and Skittles from the vending machine at school. *But I had that stew. With Jeremy. That was good stew,* Meena thinks. *When was that? What day was that? I can't even remember. What is* wrong *with me? How can I not even remember the day?* Then it hits her. It's Friday. Which means an entire weekend at home with Steven and Lydia. Meena curls in a little tighter, the waistband of her jeans cutting into her skin.

"Meena, please talk to me. Are you eating at all? Are you sleeping?" Lansky takes a deep breath and lets it out slowly. She hears him scratch at the hairs on his chin.

Meena hasn't looked directly at Dr. Lansky since she sat down. She can't stop her eyes from darting around the room—lamp, plant, spider on the wall, lamp, plant—any more than she can stop her brain from racing. "You need my help, Meena. Why won't you let me help you? All you have to do is open up to me."

Open up. Open up. Open up.

"Talk to me, Meena," he says. "You can trust me."

Meena's gaze shoots directly to his face and Lansky's head actually snaps back as if she's shot at him. That is exactly what Steven always said to her. That she could trust him. That the only people they could trust in this world were each other. Meena feels like her insides are curling in on themselves and rotting.

"What is it?" Lansky asks, obviously thinking he's on to something. "Is it the word *trust* that makes you react like that? Do you not believe you can trust me?"

Meena rips her gaze from his probing eyes and focuses on a crack in the wall above and a few feet behind him. She wishes she could trust this man. She wishes she could just tell him everything. But she knows what will happen if she talks. He'll tell her that what has happened is a shame, but that it's all her fault. She didn't do enough to stop it. She didn't do anything. She wanted it, after all, didn't she? Didn't she want it to happen? Meena is to blame. She knows it. Steven knows it. And if she says anything, everyone will know the truth. Meena is to blame.

"Is there anyone in your life that you feel you *can* trust?" Dr. Lansky asks, ever patient. "Your parents? Your brothers? How about a friend?"

Meena's thoughts immediately flash over Dana's face. Karyn's face. Luke's face. They finally land on Peter Davis's face. And for some reason, they stay there.

Earlier that week in the nurse's office and then at the diner, she'd said more to him than she'd said to pretty much anyone else in an entire week. Jeremy had tried, but she couldn't talk to him the way she had talked to Peter. Jeremy's too close to her old life. Too much a part of her crowd and all the things she's lost. But Peter . . . . Peter is different somehow. Safer. She remembers his face. The lack of disappointment in his eyes. She wishes she could talk to him. Suddenly wishes it with an incredible ferocity, even though they haven't been friends in so long. But she knows she won't. Not now. Not even soon. Maybe never. Maybe she will never talk to anyone ever again.

Dr. Lansky continues to ask his level questions, assured that sooner or later, Meena will finally open her soul. But the longer she sits there, the further she withdraws.

I have to get out of here. I have to get out. . . .

• • •

Jeremy's parents came home over an hour ago. No one has ventured up to his room to say hello. No one has acknowledged his presence in the house at all. As Jeremy pulls on his long black coat and checks himself over in the mirror, he makes a decision. If they're going to ignore him, he's going to ignore them. As much as he wants to talk this through with his parents and come to some kind of understanding, as much as he wants this brokenhearted feeling to go away and wants to tell them about what happened at school today and have them comfort him and listen to him, he realizes now that they're not ready. And they may never be ready. That's just something he'll have to deal with.

He checks out his costume quickly. He's decided to go as Angel after all. It was the only thing he could do just by raiding his closet. He's wearing black pants, a plain dark blue shirt, and black shoes. His hair is gelled up appropriately. Yep. He could be a vampire. Jeremy smirks involuntarily. His parents would probably be happier if he *was* a creature of the night instead of just a guy who's attracted to other guys.

Jeremy is already down the stairs and has one hand on the doorknob when someone finally talks to him.

"Where are you going?" his father asks, walking into the foyer as he dries his hands on a kitchen towel. His eyes flick over Jeremy's outfit and he registers surprise. Jeremy grips the doorknob harder when he realizes his father is thinking that this is the way Jeremy is going to be dressing now that he's gay.

"A Halloween party, Dad," Jeremy says sarcastically. "This is my costume."

"Where is this party? And who's going to be there?" his father asks, moving his hands to his hips. "What do you think, you don't have to tell us where you're going?"

Jeremy actually laughs, his mouth dropping open in surprise. "I never have before," he says, pushing his hands into the deep pockets of his coat. "If there's a new set of rules, you'd better tell me now."

"Hey, watch it," his father says. His jaw is squared, his shoulders rolled back, and his eyes flash. "Since when do you talk to me that way?"

"Since you turned into the morality police!" Jeremy yells. He's surprised by how loudly his voice echoes off the walls but gratified by the shock that crosses his father's face.

He hears his mother's shoes clicking across the kitchen floor and she enters the foyer behind his dad. Her face is scrunched up in nervous concern. "Keep it down!" she hisses, one chunk of red hair falling out of the twist at the back of her head. "Emily is in her room!"

"Look," Jeremy's father snaps loudly, too angry to really heed his wife's warning. "This is not the life I envisioned for you—"

"Oh, that's such a cop-out!" Jeremy shouts, throwing his hands in the air and letting them slap back down at his sides. "Do you think this is the life I envisioned for myself? Do you think I want people laughing at me, vandalizing my stuff . . . threatening me? Yeah, I've *really*

179

been looking forward to being a total outcast! I did not ask for this!"

His last shout seems to reverberate throughout the house and Jeremy hears the door to his sister's room squeak open. His father takes a long breath and speaks through his teeth.

"And I didn't ask for a son who would speak to me so disrespectfully," he says, glaring at Jeremy.

He doesn't tell his father he's missing the big picture here. He has a feeling that comment would get him drop-kicked right out of the house.

"I'm sorry for yelling," Jeremy says quietly as his sister comes jogging down the stairs, her little footsteps almost noiseless. She reaches the middle landing and leans into the banister.

"What's going on?" she asks shakily.

"Not now, Emily!" his father roars, snapping again. Emily bursts into tears and runs back upstairs, slamming her bedroom door behind her. Jeremy wants to go after her, but he stands his ground. He has a feeling he needs to finish this now or it's never going to end. His mother climbs the stairs to go after her daughter and Jeremy looks at his dad. Maybe he'll chill out a little now that he's lost it on Emily for no good reason.

"I just have one question," his father says, moving his weight from one foot to the other and crossing his arms over his chest. "Is *he* going to be there?"

Jeremy feels like he's been slapped. He even pulls his head back from the force of the accusation in the question his father has just asked. A few moments pass before he can answer.

"Do you mean Josh?" he asks. "You want to know if *Josh* is going to be there?"

His father just lifts his chin slightly and Jeremy knows he's right.

"You know what?" Jeremy whispers harshly. "You would not be giving me this crap if I had kissed some random girl. You would have told me to have a great night and sent me on my way." He takes a few steps closer to his father and looks him directly in the face. "This is bull, Dad. And I think that somewhere deep down, you know you're wrong. And I think it pisses you off."

His father blinks a few times but otherwise doesn't move a muscle. "I've had just about enough of this," he says.

"Yeah? Me too," Jeremy says, brushing past his father. "So I'm going to do us both a favor."

Shaking with anger and adrenaline, Jeremy takes the steps two at a time to his bedroom. He yanks his big duffel bag out from under his bed and starts stuffing clothes into it. Half his underwear drawer. Socks. A few shirts. A couple of pairs of jeans. On his way back to the stairs, he goes into the bathroom and grabs his toothbrush. When he gets back down to the foyer, his father is standing exactly where he left him.

"I'm outta here," Jeremy says as he pulls his bag up on his shoulder. He can't believe it's come to this, but he knows he's going to have a hard enough time accepting his new life. His new self. He can't spend one more minute in this house with parents who are supposed to love him treating him like he's a freak of nature. He opens the front door and turns to take a last look at his father. "And don't wait up, because I'm not coming back."

The door slam feels good, but it's only temporary. As Jeremy climbs into his car and starts the engine, he knows that once he leaves the party, he doesn't exactly have a place to stay tonight. But anyplace has to be better than here.

Trying to ignore the heaviness in his chest, Jeremy pulls out into the street and hits the gas. He only looks in the rearview mirror once.